MEET THE GIRL TALK CHARACTERS

Sabrina Wells is petite, with curly auburn hair, sparkling hazel eyes, and a bubbly personality. Sabrina loves magazines, shopping, sleepovers, and most of all, she loves talking to her best friends.

Katie Campbell's a straight-A student and super athlete. With her blond hair, blue eyes, and matching clothes, she's everyone's idea of little miss perfect. But Katie has a few surprises for everyone, including herself!

Randy Zak has just moved to Acorn Falls from New York City, and is she ever cool! With her 'radical' spiked haircut and her hip New York clothes, Randy teaches everyone just how much fun it is to be different.

Allison Cloud is a Native American Indian. Allison's super smart and really beautiful. But she has one major problem: She's thirteen years old, five foot seven, and still growing!

Here's what they're talking about in
Girl Talk

SABRINA: Way to go, Katie! I bet you're totally psyched about being on the Winter Carnival Synchronized Skating team!

KATIE: Well, I was excited until I found out that Laurel Spencer is going to be my skating partner. Now I don't know what to think.

SABRINA: Yeah, I guess it is pretty weird to end up having Stacy the great's *best* friend as your skating partner!

KATIE: And that's not all. Coach O'Neal wants us to really get to know each other. He says it will help our skating.

SABRINA: You mean Coach O'Neal wants you to become best friends with Laurel Spencer?!

PEER PRESSURE

By L. E. Blair

GIRL TALK® series created by Western Publishing Company, Inc.

Produced by Angel Entertainment, Inc.

Western Publishing Company, Inc., Racine, Wisconsin 53404

 Library of Congress Catalog Card Number: 90-82559 ISBN: 0-307-22009-5   C D E F G H I J K L M

Text by Cathy Lasry

Chapter One

When I opened my eyes on Friday morning, my first thought was: *Today is the day! Today I'll find out if I've made the Winter Carnival Olympic team.* Once a year the whole county gets together for a miniversion of the Winter Olympics with a huge carnival mixed in. All the schools have their own teams for the Olympic events. I had tried out for the synchronized skating team.

I looked at the clock on the white night table next to my bed. It wasn't even six o'clock yet, but I was too excited to sleep. I threw back my blue-and-white-flowered comforter and practically jumped out of bed, knocking my cat, Pepper, onto the blue rug.

After my shower I blew my hair dry and then decided to put it in a French braid, since I had so much time. I put on my favorite outfit — a blue pullover sweater and a pair of win-

1

ter-white corduroy pants. I tied a matching blue ribbon on the end of my braid and I was all set to go. The only problem was that it was six-forty-five. School didn't start until eight-thirty.

I heard a knock on the door and my sister, who I call "Princess Emily," walked into my room. She was wearing her cute pink-and-white-striped nightshirt and matching leggings.

"I thought I heard you moving around," Emily said, yawning and leaning against my doorframe. "But I had to get up and see for myself."

I shrugged and opened my English book. "I woke up early, that's all." I didn't really want to tell Emily how nervous I was. She's always so sure of herself, which is why I call her "Princess Emily." She's popular, smart, beautiful, and has a gorgeous boyfriend named Reed. And she would never even think about doing something radical, like joining the boys' ice hockey team, the way I did earlier this year.

"That's right. They announce the results from the tryouts today, don't they," Emily said with a smile. She ran her fingers through her hair, which is blond like mine, but longer and wavier. "I can understand why you're worried."

"What's that supposed to mean?" I asked, wrinkling my forehead in concern.

"I just meant that the competition is really tough this year," Emily replied.

"I was good enough to make the finals," I told her abruptly.

"Katie, I never said you weren't!" Emily said loudly, taking a step into my room. "I just thought you might be a little nervous and I wanted to help."

"Thanks," I replied, cutting her off. I was always doing that to Emily. I never meant to, but sometimes Emily acted like she was my mother instead of my sister. I turned back to my English book and stared at the pages.

"Katie, I . . ." Emily began and then stopped. She was quiet for a minute and then she left my room and walked down the hall to the bathroom. I kept staring at my English book, but all of the words started blurring together until they looked like black squiggles. *If she had really wanted to help me*, I thought to myself, *she would have wished me luck instead of telling me how tough the competition is. I know all about the competition.*

I gave up on English, packed my books, and went downstairs to the kitchen. Mom was standing by the stove, making scrambled eggs.

"Hi, Mom," I said, sitting down at the table.

"Good morning," my mother said, smiling. She walked over to the table with the frying pan and spooned some eggs onto my plate. "There's juice in the refrigerator and the toast will be ready in a second." Mom is very big on eating a balanced breakfast every day. I didn't even try to tell her that I was too nervous to eat.

"Emily!" my mother called, putting the frying pan back on the stove. "You're going to be late!"

"Here I am," Emily said, breezing into the room. She was wearing chocolate-brown harem pants, a tan sweater, and brown leather half boots. She looked really good, as usual.

Emily sat down at the table. Mom spooned some eggs onto her plate, then sat down to eat her own breakfast and read the newspaper. I gulped down my eggs and jumped up from the table. I couldn't bear to sit still. I was too excited. It was definitely time to get moving and go to school.

Mom looked up from her newspaper and frowned at me. "What's the hurry? You haven't had any juice."

Emily was watching me, too. She knew that I hadn't told Mom about the tryouts yet.

"Well, we're having an assembly during first period. Mr. Hansen's announcing the names of the Winter Carnival Olympic team," I explained. "I don't want to be late."

"Olympic team?" my mother asked, raising her eyebrows.

"Yeah, you know. They always have Olympic games at the Winter Carnival." I pulled on my coat and then looked at my watch. "Wow, I've got to get going. See you later."

I walked as fast as I could through the snow, hoping to get a really good seat for the assembly. When I got to school, I put my jacket and most of my books in the locker I share with one of my best friends, Sabrina Wells. Then I hurried toward the auditorium. There were only about ten other people there when I arrived, so I saved four seats at the end of a row in the center section and sat down to wait for my best friends — Sabrina, Allison Cloud, and Randy Zak.

At eight-fifteen, Al and Randy walked in together. I had to smile when I saw them. They are so different! Allison is a Native American, a Chippewa, and she's tall, quiet, and beautiful, with tons of long black hair. Randy's hair is black, too, but she is definitely not quiet. She's from New York, she wears black all the time, and she's always doing something to stir things up.

By eight-twenty-five, the auditorium was packed. The three of us were looking all over for Sabs, who is always late.

"There she is!" I said, catching sight of her long, curly red hair. But there was so much noise and there were so many people moving around that Sabrina couldn't see us. Randy bounced to her feet in her baggy black parachute pants and started waving her arms in the air. Then she stuck two fingers in her mouth and whistled really loud. "Hey, Sabs! Over here!"

Sabrina's head turned toward us and she smiled and waved back. A lot of other people turned and looked, too.

"Hi, guys! Sorry I'm late," Sabrina gasped when she finally reached us. "Mark wouldn't let me into the bathroom until practically seven-thirty, and then Dad said it was my turn to take out the garbage. I ended up having to run all the way here!"

Sabs is the youngest — and the only girl — of five kids. Her twin brother, Sam, was born only four minutes before her, and he never lets her forget it.

Sabs plopped down next to Randy in the aisle seat. "I think it's great that they decided to have assembly during first period. I get to miss math! Has it started yet?"

"No," Allison told her, motioning to the stage. "I think you're just in time."

I looked toward the front of the auditorium. Mr. Hansen, the principal of Bradley Junior High, was walking up the stairs and onto the stage. He was holding a couple of sheets of paper in his left hand and kept adjusting his tie with the other hand as he crossed in front of the curtain to the podium.

"Good morning, students," Mr. Hansen began. "As I'm sure you all know, we have called this assembly to announce the names of the Bradley Junior High Winter Carnival Olympic team."

Lots of people started cheering, including me. Finally, I would find out if I had made it! I had to sit on my hands to keep from clapping furiously.

"Good luck, Katie," Allison whispered. She reached over and squeezed my shoulder. I smiled at her nervously. Allison, Randy, and Sabrina had been rooting for me ever since I told them I was going to try out for the team.

As Mr. Hansen began to read off the list of names, Sabs started bouncing up and down in her seat. She looked even more excited than I felt! Randy glanced in my direction and gave me a thumbs-up sign.

Mr. Hansen was reading the team list in alphabetical order by event and there was a long way to go before he got to synchronized skating, so I started worrying about my try-outs again. Sure, I was a finalist, but only about four of the finalists would actually make it onto the team.

The tryouts had seemed pretty easy while I was in the middle of them last week. I kept remembering what it had been like to try out for the boys' ice hockey team at the beginning of the school year. Back then, I'd had a lot more to worry about than just my skating ability. None of the boys on the team had wanted to have a girl ice hockey player around, so they were really hard on me during scrimmages and drills. Even the coach had tried to discourage me from playing at first. But I didn't let them stop me. I made the team and even helped scored a goal during my very first game!

The Winter Carnival tryouts were a whole different kind of skating, though. Synchronized skating uses lots of figure skating moves, like jumps and turns. I taught myself how to figure skate by watching television and then practicing until I thought I had the moves down right. Emily used to tell me I was crazy to even try some of the stuff I did. She said I didn't know what I was doing and I'd only end up hurting myself. Luckily, I never did.

"Katie," Allison whispered into my ear. "Are you listening? Mr. Hansen's started on the skating events."

I shook my head to clear it. "Thanks, Al," I

whispered back. I sat up in my seat. It was a little hard to hear Mr. Hansen over the voices of the students around me as they talked about the Olympic team, congratulating friends who had made it and cheering up the ones who had been cut. I tried to tune them out.

". . . and Connie Sanderson. Once again, that's the figure skating team. Next comes speed skating. The team members will be: Michael Davis, Kevin Caran, Peter Jemilo, Drew Schwartz, Scott Silver, Philip Walsh, and Brian Williams."

I smiled. Most of the guys Mr. Hansen had named were friends of mine from the hockey team.

"Now we come to a new event, synchronized skating," the principal went on. "The two pairs will be Stacy Hansen with Kim Kushner and Katie Campbell . . . ."

For a second, I was sure that I was going to float right out of my seat and up to the ceiling. I was on the synchronized skating team! I had made it! I was so incredibly excited that I jumped out of my seat, hugged Sabrina, Randy, and Allison, and sat down again. For the rest of the assembly, I just sat there with a big smile on my face.

Mr. Hansen dismissed us just as the bell rang, announcing the end of first period. I gathered up my books and practically skipped to the door.

"Hey, guys! What's wrong?" I asked, looking at their solemn expressions. "Didn't you hear? I made it! I'm on the synchronized skating team!"

Randy looked at Al, Al looked at Sabs, and Sabs looked at me, her blue eyes wide.

"Aren't you even happy for me?" I said, looking them in the eye one by one. None of us paid any attention to the crowds of kids streaming past us in the hallway.

"Of course we're happy for you," Allison said uncertainly, glancing down at her shoes.

"I guess we just didn't expect you to take the news this well," Randy added. She ran a hand through her thick black hair, making the top stand on end.

"I'm sorry," Sabrina blurted out.

"Sorry?" I asked, totally confused. "What are you talking about? I made it onto the team. Only four girls in the whole school made it — Kim Kushner, Stacy Hansen, me, and my partner, whoever she is."

"You didn't hear?" Sabrina gasped, raising her eyebrows.

"No," I told her, laughing. "I was so excited after I heard my own name that I didn't even listen to the rest of the announcement."

"Al, I think you should tell her," Randy said.

"Yeah," Sabs agreed, nodding her head so hard that a few of her red curls escaped from the red combs she was using to hold them back from her face.

"Okay," Allison said quietly and then took a deep breath. "Katie, I'm really sorry, but Mr. Hansen said your partner is . . ." She hesitated. "Laurel Spencer."

Laurel Spencer! My jaw dropped open and my feet felt as if they were glued to the floor. There had to be a mistake! Laurel Spencer is one of the richest girls at school. Her best friend is Stacy Hansen, the principal's daughter. Both of them are really stuck-up. I guess because Laurel has money and Stacy has a principal for a father, they think it makes them really special or something.

My best friend back in sixth grade, Erica

Dunn, used to be friends with Stacy and Laurel, and every once in a while they would ask me to go with them to the mall or something. But I never felt all that comfortable around them, especially Laurel, since she and Erica had been best friends before Erica started being friends with me.

Ever since Erica moved to California last summer, Stacy and Laurel have acted as if they never knew me. I don't mind at all. I like Randy, Sabs, and Allison a whole lot better than those snobs.

Of all the girls at Bradley, how could they possibly have paired me up with Laurel Spencer? It almost made me wish that I'd never even learned how to skate.

Chapter Two

"Oh, my gosh! I completely forgot to tell you!" Sabrina exclaimed while we were sitting at lunch later that day.

"What is it?" Allison asked, smiling at Sabs's enthusiasm.

"Hi, guys," Randy called as she walked up to our table. She took off her black leather jacket, hung it over the back of her chair, and sat down.

"Oh, good," Sabs said. "Now I can tell all of you at once. Remember when I had those band tryouts for the Winter Carnival band?"

"Sure," I answered, forcing myself to smile. "You wouldn't go to Fitzie's with us after school or anything for a whole week because you wanted to practice."

"Right." Sabrina nodded and took a sip of her milk. "Well, Mr. Metcalf, the band leader, asked me to stay after class for a minute today.

14

He told me that I made the band! And he wants me to be first clarinet!"

"That's terrific, Sabs!" Allison exclaimed.

"Yeah, that's great," I said, trying to sound excited. I couldn't stop thinking that I was not going to have any fun at the carnival with Laurel Spencer as my skating partner.

"I guess I'll see you at rehearsals, then," Randy put in calmly. She spooned up some more of her banana yogurt.

"What?" Sabs asked, looking totally confused.

"I tried out for the percussion section," Randy answered with a grin. "Mr. Metcalf said it didn't matter that I wasn't in the school band. I stopped by his office on my way to lunch and he told me that I made it, too."

"Wow! That's awesome!" Sabrina's eyes were shining, and she was talking so fast that I could hardly tell where one word ended and the next began. "We can go to all the practices together and everything. Isn't it great? Now we're all doing something at the Winter Carnival."

Suddenly, Sabrina's hand flew up to cover her mouth. Her face turned bright red as she

15

looked over at Allison.

"Oh, Al. I'm sorry," Sabs apologized. "I'm sure that next year . . ."

"It's okay, Sabs." Allison smiled reassuringly. "I haven't had the chance to tell you *my* good news yet. I'm one of the school reporters for the Winter Carnival Olympics," Allison replied quietly.

"Congratulations!" I said, really happy for Al.

"Yeah, that's cool, Al," said Randy with a big smile. She and Al are really close.

"Thanks." Allison blushed and started fiddling with her fork. "I'm a little nervous about it, though."

"Why? You're an awesome writer," Randy insisted.

"I'm just worried about talking to all those kids and coaches and stuff. You know," Allison said.

Allison is a very quiet person, and she's kind of shy until you get to know her. She probably figured it would be hard to just walk up to people and start asking them questions. But I had a feeling she'd be good at it.

"Come on, Al," Randy encouraged. "Most

of the people you'll be talking to are kids, just like us. What could be so hard about that?"

Sometimes I wonder how Allison and Randy got to be such good friends. They are so totally different. Randy is the last person on Earth who I would ever call shy. Maybe it's because she grew up in New York City.

"I know they're just kids," Allison said quietly, "but I'm still nervous."

"You probably feel a lot like I did when I tried out for the boys' hockey team," I told her. *Or like I feel about having Laurel Spencer as a synchronized skating partner*, I thought. I picked at the spaghetti on my tray. It's usually my favorite, but I didn't feel like eating any more.

"Yeah! If Katie could do something like that, then you can definitely do those interviews," Sabs chimed in enthusiastically. "Hey! Maybe you'll even get to do a story about Katie!"

"Ms. Staats said that she really wanted one of the articles to be about synchronized skating, since it's a new sport," Al told her, nodding.

"Isn't it something one of the skating instructors at the rink came up with?" Sabrina questioned.

"Uh-huh," I replied. "Her name is Katherine Stuart. She used to be a professional pair skater. Her partner hurt his leg in a fall or something a couple of years ago, so she retired and started teaching skating instead. She got the idea from synchronized swimming. Two people skate together, trying to do exactly the same movements at the same time. They dress alike and wear their hair the same way and everything. I think Mrs. Stuart wants it to be a carnival event so that other people hear about it, too." I had fallen in love with the whole idea of synchronized skating from the very first time I had heard about it.

"It sounds like a lot of fun," Sabrina said.

"It sounds like a lot of work, too," Randy added. She was scraping the last of her yogurt from the sides of the container.

Allison looked concerned. "You really have to know your partner well, don't you, Katie? I mean, to skate in sync like that?"

I nodded miserably. "We're supposed to be like mirror images of each other. I don't know how I can possibly do that with Laurel. We're so . . . so . . ."

"Different," Randy finished for me.

"Totally," Sabs added.

I stood up to carry my tray to the dishwasher's window. I dropped it off and turned around to go back to my table.

"Hello, Katie," a girl's voice said from behind me.

I whirled around. It was Laurel.

"Um . . . hi," I replied, flustered. I didn't know what to do. No matter how I felt about Laurel, she was still my partner for the Olympics. If we didn't start getting along, we'd never be able to skate together. "So," I went on, clasping my hands in front of me. "I guess we're going to be partners for synchronized skating."

"Mmmm," Laurel murmured, looking away from me for a second and tossing her beautiful, wavy light brown hair behind her shoulders, just like Stacy Hansen always does.

What was that "Mmmm" supposed to mean? I was trying to be nice about this. Laurel didn't seem to realize that, though.

"I wanted to talk to you about that," Laurel went on, looking me up and down. I began to wish I was more dressed up or something.

Laurel is one of those people who always look terrific and her clothes are super-sophisticated. Like, today she was wearing a navy-blue pleated wool skirt, a white blouse, and a blue wool jacket. "Aren't you just a hockey player? I mean, you've never had any figure skating lessons or anything, have you?"

"Well, I . . ." I stammered. I didn't know what to say. I had to admit that she was right. I hadn't really taken skating lessons. My dad had taught me a lot, but I'd picked up the rest on my own. Still, I knew I was a good skater. After all, I had gotten picked for the team. And a lot of the other girls at the tryouts had been taking lessons for years.

"I'm only asking because I know what a nice person you are," Laurel went on in a fake sweet voice, her nose in the air. "I know you wouldn't want Bradley to lose the synchronized skating event because you can't skate as well as the rest of us. So, if you want to tell Coach O'Neal that you've changed your mind about being on the team . . ."

Laurel's voice trailed off. She smiled at me coldly, her blue eyes hard, and turned away. I stood there for a second, biting my lip so that I wouldn't cry. Then I started to get angry. So Laurel Spencer didn't think I was good enough, did she? Well, I'd show her! I was going to be the best synchronized skating partner in the whole world! And if Bradley Junior High didn't win the gold medal, it wasn't going to be because of me.

"Katie!" Randy said when I got back to our table. "We saw Laurel walk up to you by the dishwasher's window. Was she her usual 'Ice Queen' self?"

"Sort of," I answered, pretending to be searching for a book in my knapsack so I didn't have to look at my friends. I didn't want them to see how upset I was. If Randy found out what Laurel had really said, she'd probably go over to her and start a fight or something. Randy is like that. She always stands up for anyone she feels is being picked on, especially one of her best friends.

"Well, what did she say?" Sabrina asked.

"Oh, we were just talking about skating and the carnival," I replied, trying to act as casual as possible.

"Did she say anything about you two being partners?" Sabs persisted.

I sighed. "She just said she hoped I could figure-skate as well as I play hockey," I finally said.

"Katie!" Sabs gasped. "How could she say that?" Sabs is the most loyal friend in the world.

"That is absolutely the most rotten thing I've ever heard," Randy practically growled, her dark eyes flashing with anger. "What does she think — that you're not good enough to skate with her?"

"It could have been a compliment," Allison jumped in quickly.

"A compliment?" Randy asked, wrinkling her forehead skeptically.

"Sure," Allison said, nodding. "Katie's a really great hockey player. Everybody knows that. Laurel probably just meant that they'll have a good chance of winning if Katie is as good at figure skating as she is at hockey." Al always thinks the best of people. But she hadn't seen Laurel's eyes.

"I don't know," Randy said, glowering at something over my shoulder. I turned to see what it was.

"Poor Laurel," Stacy said loudly as she

passed our table. "I feel so bad that she got stuck with that tomboy Katie Campbell as her partner for the carnival. I mean, she's an ice hockey player, not a figure skater. She'll probably wear hockey skates."

"Sounds to me like Katie's the one who's stuck," Randy muttered.

"What did you say?" Stacy demanded, her face flushing red. She put her hand on her hip and flicked her long golden hair over her shoulder.

"Randy, I don't think — " I began.

"Go ahead and stick up for your friend, Randy Zak," Stacy shrilled. "Then I can laugh at you after she makes a fool out of herself at the Olympics!" Stacy turned to me. "And as for you, Katie Campbell, you'd better not make Laurel look bad!"

Make Laurel look bad? Now I was furious. As the bell rang and we all started into the hallway toward our next classes, I made a solemn vow to myself. I was going to get through this no matter what Laurel Spencer and Stacy Hansen said — and if they looked bad, it was not going to be my fault!

Chapter Three

School seemed to drag on forever. At last, the three o'clock bell rang. Each of the Olympic team members had to pick up a copy of the practice schedule from the principal's office. I decided to stop by my locker first, to get my jacket and the rest of my books. That way I could leave straight from there.

"Hey, Katie!" someone called from behind me as I stood in front of my locker. I turned around and saw Randy walking toward me. She was wearing her Walkman and I could hear the music from two feet away. It was some kind of heavy-duty rock and roll.

"Hi, Ran," I said loudly. I got my jacket out of my locker and started pulling out the books I would need to do my homework. "What's up?"

"We have a band meeting at three-forty-five," she explained, pulling her headphones off, "so I'm going to be hanging around here for a while. I can't figure out why they decided to have us meet forty-five minutes after school is over."

"They're probably having a chorus rehearsal first, or something," I guessed. I closed and locked the door to my locker. "Want to come to the principal's office with me? I have to pick up my schedule," I continued, bending down to pull up my sock. I hate it when one of my socks is pulled up higher than the other. It makes me feel lopsided.

"Sure. I need a copy, too." Randy and I walked down the crowded hallway. When we reached the principal's office, there were a few other people waiting to pick up schedules. As we stepped onto the end of the short line, I groaned. Randy, who was listening to her Walkman again, didn't notice until I tapped her on the shoulder. When she saw who I was pointing at, her dark eyes started flashing again.

Just ahead of us, Stacy and Laurel were waiting to pick up their rehearsal schedules. I wanted to let a few people get in front of me so I could avoid them, but it was too late. They had already seen us.

"Laurel, look who's here," Stacy said, putting her hands on her hips and aiming an all-teeth, totally fake smile at me.

Laurel turned and looked at me. She didn't smile, but she didn't make a face, either. I couldn't tell what she was thinking at all.

"Actually, I'm glad we ran into you," Stacy continued, still pretending to smile. "We just thought you'd like to know that we're asking Coach O'Neal to switch partners around so that Laurel and I can be together. Of course, it's only because Laurel and I already know each other so well. We figured it would be better to have at least one pair of skaters who weren't practically strangers. You understand," Stacy concluded smugly. I didn't know what to say. She was right — in a way.

"You know, Stacy," Randy said suddenly in a voice so sickeningly sweet that I had to look at her before I could believe that it was actually her talking, "I think that's one of the best ideas I've ever heard."

I stared at Randy in surprise. I'd never thought I would ever hear her say something nice to Stacy Hansen!

"After all, it only makes sense to match up the skaters by how talented they are. We all know how good Kim Kushner is — she's won tons of awards for her figure skating. So I think you're absolutely right to say that Katie should be matched with someone who's her equal in terms of talent! Don't you think so, Katie?" Randy finished, still speaking in that strange, sweet voice.

"Absolutely," I said firmly, trying hard not to laugh.

At first, Stacy just kept on smiling. Then, as what Randy had said sunk in, her face turned chalk white and her nostrils flared.

While Stacy and Randy were eyeing each other, I quickly walked to the front desk, picked up two copies of the schedule, and hurried back to Randy's side. I tried not to look at Laurel at all. I knew that it would probably be best if Stacy did manage to talk Coach O'Neal into changing the teams around. I mean, I didn't know Kim Kushner that well, but I was pretty sure that she'd be easier to work with than Laurel.

All I really knew about Kim was that she was a smart, pretty eighth grader who had been winning trophies and awards in figure skating since she was about ten years old. She had shoulder-length brown hair, brown eyes, and a great figure.

I handed Randy her copy of the schedule.

"Thanks," she said, still looking at Stacy.

"I think we'd better go," I said, pulling gently on her arm.

"Okay," Randy replied. She grinned widely at Stacy and Laurel as we walked out the door. "Bye, girls! Good luck."

As soon as we walked out the office door, Randy started roaring with laughter.

"That was the most fun I've had in a long time," she gasped. "Did you see Stacy's face?"

"Randy, you're the only person I know who can make Stacy that mad," I said, laughing.

"It was fun," Randy said, still laughing.

I said good-bye to Randy and started home. It had gotten a lot colder since the morning and there was ice all over the sidewalks. I tried to skate along the bigger patches, but boots are really not meant to be used as ice skates. It was fun anyway. I love skating in any way, shape, or form.

It was almost four o'clock when I finally

got home.

"Mom?" I called. "I'm home." I walked through the living room and into the kitchen. Mom was sitting at the kitchen table, talking to someone on the telephone. Part of the reason my mother likes working at the bank is that she gets to come home at three o'clock on Mondays, Wednesdays, and Fridays. Mom smiled and waved at me. I waved back and walked over to the refrigerator to get some milk. I poured myself a glass and then took a couple of oatmeal raisin cookies from the jar on the counter near the sink. Oatmeal raisin cookies are my favorite.

"Hi, Katie," Mom finally said when she hung up the phone. "How was your day?"

"Pretty good. I have some awesome news. Mom, I made the Winter Carnival Olympic synchronized skating team!" The words came out all in a rush.

"Well," she said after a few moments of total silence. "Congratulations, honey. Emily told me how important it was to you to make the team."

I smiled at her. I knew she didn't quite understand why I liked skating, so it must have been hard for her to say that.

"Yeah," I said, even more enthusiastically. "I couldn't believe it when Mr. Hansen called my name. It was . . ."

"Hello! Anybody home?" a voice shouted.

It was Emily. She sounded really excited about something.

"We're here, in the kitchen, Em," my mother called out.

Emily came rushing in, breathless. She still had her jacket on. That wasn't like her at all. She's always very neat.

"Mom! Katie! You're not going to believe this! It's absolutely incredible!"

My mom smiled. "What's 'absolutely incredible?'"

Emily was beaming. "I've been chosen as the Winter Carnival Queen for Bradley Senior High! Can you believe it?"

"Oh, Emily! That's wonderful!" my mother exclaimed, standing up to give my sister a hug. "So tell me, what do you have to do?"

Emily took off her jacket and hung it over the back of her chair, something that Mom never allows us to do. She sat down and they started talking about the dress Emily would have to have. I got up and put my glass in the sink and started to walk away.

"Katie, where are you going?" Emily asked. She sounded surprised that I was leaving the kitchen in the middle of her big news.

"Oh, I'm just going out to shovel the front walk before it freezes any more." Whenever I'm feeling a little down, exercise always helps make me feel better, so right about now, shoveling the sidewalk sounded pretty good.

"That's a good idea, Katie," my mother said with a smile. "But before you go, I want you to know that I'm proud of both of my girls." She gave me a big smile and then turned back to Emily. "So, Emily dear, what colors are you thinking about for your dress?"

I walked into the hall and pulled on a pair of boots and my jacket. I grabbed a shovel and started attacking the snow and ice in front of my house.

Chapter Four

The next morning was Saturday. It was also the synchronized skating team's first official practice. We were meeting at ten o'clock at the indoor rink where the hockey team plays.

After I had looked through my closet twice without finding anything to wear, I decided to ask Emily if I could borrow something of hers. Emily is really into clothes, and she's got tons of them in all different styles.

I walked across the hall and knocked on Emily's door.

"Come in," she said.

Emily was sitting Indian-style on top of her white eyelet comforter with a copy of *Belle* in her lap. She was wearing a pale pink terry-cloth bathrobe and her hair was pulled up into a ponytail.

"Em, I was wondering if I could borrow something to wear to my skating practice," I ventured.

"Sure," she said. "There's a really nice light green miniskirt on that side of the closet." She pointed to the right side of her walk-in closet. "It's a little bit small on me, anyway. Go ahead. You can have it, if you want."

"Thanks," I said, surprised.

I found the skirt and started walking back to my room to finish dressing.

"Katie," Emily called after me.

"Yeah?" I looked back over my shoulder.

"Congratulations on making the team. I know you'll do a great job."

"I . . . thanks, Em," I murmured. "And congratulations to you, too. You'll be the most beautiful Winter Carnival Queen that Acorn Falls has ever seen." Feeling kind of embarrassed, I slipped back into my own room and shut the door.

When I finally finished dressing, I was wearing a pair of white wool leggings, the pale green miniskirt, and a long-sleeved, green-and- white-striped T-shirt. I pulled my hair back into a ponytail tied with a light green ribbon, to keep it out of my face when I was skating. I wished that I could wear a pair of earrings or some makeup, but my mom didn't think I was old enough yet. Still, I thought I looked pretty good.

I ran downstairs, grabbed my skates and jacket, and yelled good-bye to my mother. It was a beautiful, sunny day, and all the ice had melted into little puddles, but it was still cold enough for me to see my breath in the air.

I ran all the way to the rink to warm myself up. When I got there, Stacy and Laurel were already on the ice. I sat down on the bleachers and laced up my skates, watching the two of them out of the corner of my eye.

I could tell that both Stacy and Laurel had taken a lot of figure skating lessons. Laurel's skating was very exact and polished, but she was concentrating so hard that she looked kind of stiff. She didn't even smile.

Stacy was totally different. Every move she made was overdone and dramatic. I noticed that she kept doing the same basic jumps and turns over and over again, waving her arms and smiling hugely the whole time.

Both of them were dressed in expensive-looking skating outfits. Laurel's was simple and elegant, just a navy-blue leotard and skating skirt, flesh-colored stockings, and flesh-colored skates like the professionals have. Stacy was wearing a bright purple skirt with a matching purple-and-white sweater. She even had purple pom-poms on her skates!

I took a deep breath and awkwardly walked across the rubber floormats on the to the ice in my well-worn, dirty white skates. I wondered if Stacy and Laurel had spoken to Coach O'Neal about switching partners. I figured he would let us know soon enough if they had.

I started doing some of the simple figures that my dad had taught me to warm up my legs and feet. I skated in a big figure eight at one end of the rink, switching directions and skates every once in a while, and concentrating on going over the same line I had first traced on the ice. Stacy and Laurel totally ignored me. When Kim came on the ice a few minutes later, she nodded a hello.

At ten o'clock on the dot, Coach O'Neal arrived. He blew his whistle and signaled for the four of us to gather around him.

"I'm glad to see you here, girls. I don't have to tell you how excited I am about the addition of this new event to our Winter Carnival Olympics. From seeing you in tryouts, I'm confident that, with a lot of hard work, we can give those other schools some really tough competition. So," the coach concluded, standing up straight and skating to the middle of the ice, "let's get started!"

I couldn't help wondering if he had decided to switch the pairs around or not when he said, "Okay. It's Stacy with Kim and Laurel with Katie. Please get together with your partners." Laurel didn't budge from where she was standing next to Stacy, so I skated over to stand on her other side.

Coach O'Neal started us out with some drills to help us learn to work together. First we had to skate side by side around the rink, turning and accelerating together each time he blew his whistle. Laurel, instead of trying to work with me, did everything she could to make the drill harder. Rather than starting with her right foot after each turn, like the coach had told us to, she kept switching feet and confusing me.

Then Coach told us to link elbows and skate backward together, trying to make our feet and legs move exactly the same way as our partner's. Laurel kept pulling on my arm, ruining my balance. I wanted to say something, but it would have made me look like I was a bad sport.

Finally, the coach blew a long blast on his whistle again and called us over.

"Well," Coach O'Neal began, first scratching his head and then rubbing his neck, "it seems we're all a bit nervous today, and I'm not really surprised. Synchronized skating is a new concept for all of us and it's going to take some time to get used to working with each other. I think what you have to do is relax and learn to trust your partner."

I almost started giggling when he said that. Laurel Spencer and I would *never* be able to do that.

"Now, I want you to meet with your partner before our next practice on — " Coach O'Neal paused to check his clipboard "on Monday. I'd like each pair to bring samples of music that they'd like to use in their routines. Each routine should be about four minutes long. I'm sure that finding the right music will help you get to know each other a little better."

The coach dismissed us and I went back to the bleachers to take off my skates . I saw Stacy and Kim talking together. Then Stacy started to laugh. I had been too busy trying to work with Laurel to notice how they had done on the ice, but it sure looked as if they were getting along all right.

"Katie?" I looked up from unlacing my skates. Laurel was standing in front of me.

"Hi," I said.

"I thought we'd better talk about when we're going to meet to choose our music," Laurel said.

"Well, it will probably have to be sometime tomorrow," I told her.

"I have a really good stereo and a lot of albums and tapes," Laurel offered. "We could meet at my house."

"Okay," I said, shrugging. "What time?"

"About one o'clock?" she suggested.

"Sure. Um . . . I already know where you live and everything, so I'll just meet you there at one."

"Fine," Laurel said. "See you." She adjusted her skate bag on her shoulder and walked straight to where Stacy was waiting for her.

I called Sabs as soon as I got home. She picked up the phone on the second ring.

"Hi! Sabs here!"

"Hi, Sabs. It's me," I said. I was sitting at the kitchen table, eating cookies. Mom was out shopping and Emily was at the mall with her friends.

"Katie!" Sabs practically screamed. "I've been waiting and waiting for you to call. How did it go? What happened with Laurel and Stacy? Were they totally obnoxious?"

"Well, not really. I mean, they didn't really say much."

"Well, I guess that's better than having an argument with them, or something," Sabs replied.

"But Laurel was still kind of . . . difficult. She didn't exactly help things go smoothly. Anyway," I said, wanting to get to the really important part, "you will never guess what the coach wants us to do."

"What?" Sabs sounded as if she was dying of curiosity.

"He said we have to pick out the music for our routine before our practice on Monday. So I'm going to Laurel's tomorrow afternoon because she says she has a great music collection."

"You're kidding!" Sabs yelled so loud that I had to hold the phone away from my ear. I giggled.

"It's not that big a deal," I told her.

"Her house is really huge," Sabrina said eagerly. "I wonder what it looks like inside. Maybe you could take a camera and . . ."

"Sabs!" I started laughing. "You know I can't do something like that!"

"Yeah, I know. Hey, why don't you come over to my house?" she asked.

"That's a great idea! I want to take a shower and change, then I'll get there around three. Why don't you call Randy and Allison, too?"

"I already did," Sabrina confessed with a laugh. "I just have to tell them what time to come over."

"Okay. See you at three," I told her.

"Bye!" Sabrina said.

As I hung up the phone I realized that I already felt better about the situation with Laurel. Talking to Sabrina always cheers me up. She's the best friend in the whole world.

Chapter Five

"Laurel Spencer's house?" Emily said, giving me a big smile at the breakfast table the next morning. "I didn't know you were friends. I remember her older sister, Lana. She's a ballerina, right?"

"I didn't even know that Laurel had an older sister, let alone that she was a ballerina," I told Emily.

"Well, I'm glad you're getting to know her," my mother commented. "You know I work for her father, Mr. Spencer, at the bank."

Laurel's father is president of the town bank. "Mom, I'm just going over to her house to pick out the music for our routine," I said to my mother. "We're not exactly friends."

"Well," Emily said, getting up, "I'm going over to Jill's house, and she lives near the Spencers. I'll drop you off."

I wiped my mouth with a napkin. "Mom,

will you be able to pick me up later?" I asked.

"Sure, honey," she replied, taking a sip of coffee. "Leave the address next to the telephone. I'll be here all day. Have a good time, and tell me all about it when I see you."

When we pulled up in front of Laurel's house, I got a sudden case of butterflies in my stomach. It was a mansion! A huge, red-brick building with columns and a long curving driveway and everything. From the car, I could see at least four chimneys, and there must have been fifty windows on the front of the house.

I said good-bye to Emily and walked quickly up to the front door and rang the bell. I half expected a butler to answer the door. But instead, it was just Laurel.

"Hi," Laurel said. "Can I take your jacket?" She wasn't being really friendly or really unfriendly. She just sounded sort of neutral, like always. I guess some people are kind of reserved and unemotional like that.

I took off my jacket and handed it to her. She hung it in this enormous closet in the hall.

"Well, why don't you come in and meet my mother and sister," Laurel continued. "Then we can go up to my room and pick out some music."

I followed her into a huge room off the foyer. The walls were all covered with flowery wallpaper, and there were fresh flowers all over the place. There was a grand piano with dozens of silver picture frames on top of it. Through the French doors behind the piano I could see two snow-covered tennis courts and a pool. It was unbelievable.

Mrs. Spencer and Laurel's sister were seated on two small white sofas in front of the fireplace, which was blazing with a beautiful fire. They were very involved in a conversation and didn't seem to notice us standing there.

"Mother," Laurel said. I was surprised. I had never heard anyone call their mother "Mother" before. It sounded so . . . formal.

Mrs. Spencer looked up with this weird expression on her face, almost as if she was annoyed. She was dressed in a beautiful cream-colored cashmere sweater and tan slacks, and her short brown hair was perfectly done. She also had on the biggest diamond ring I had ever seen, and her nails were long, red, and perfectly manicured. But she wasn't exactly pretty because of the sour expression on her face.

"Mother, this is Katie Campbell," Laurel announced in the same formal voice.

Mrs. Spencer looked me up and down before she said anything. I felt sort of self-conscious in my jeans and a red crewneck sweater. "It's very nice to meet you," she finally replied. "Are you girls working on a school project?" Even though she had asked the question, I didn't really think she was all that interested in the answer.

"Mother, I told you. Katie is my partner in the synchronized skating event for the Winter Olympics," Laurel explained in this exasperated tone of voice as if she had told her the exact same thing twenty times already. "We have to choose the music for our routine," Laurel finished.

"Oh, yes," Mrs. Spencer said, smiling this fake kind of smile. She barely seemed to have heard what Laurel had said.

"Synchronized skating?" Lana asked, looking up. "That must be new. I was on the figure skating team when I went to Bradley. I won first place both years," she added.

Laurel looked at the floor. "Lana, this is Katie," Laurel said flatly.

"Hi," I said politely with what Sabs calls my "for adults only" face. I pursed my lips a little bit and kind of raised my eyebrows and smiled all at the same time.

"Hello, Katie," Lana replied as if I were about three years old.

Lana was definitely stuck-up. I guessed she was probably in college. She was really pretty, with green eyes, pale white skin, and long black hair, which she had twisted into a bun at the nape of her neck. She was wearing a dancer's black unitard, and it was obvious from the way she was holding herself as she sat there that she was totally into ballet and wanted everyone to know it.

"We're going up to my room now," Laurel said, but Mrs. Spencer had already turned back to Lana and asked her a question. As Laurel and I walked out of the room, I couldn't help but hear some bits and pieces of their conversation. They were discussing a performance Lana had just been in near Minneapolis. From the way they were talking about it, I could tell that Lana must be a really serious dancer.

From the way Mrs. Spencer was hanging on to her every word, I could also tell that Lana was very spoiled.

I followed Laurel up a curved staircase to the second floor. When we got to the top, we walked down a thickly carpeted hallway.

I gasped when Laurel opened the door. Her room had just about everything in the world in it. It was all done in navy blue and cream, with a big canopy bed in the middle. Next to her bed was a big, old-fashioned-looking telephone that I thought was really cool. She also had the most incredible stereo system I had ever seen with whole shelves full of albums, tapes, and CDs.

Directly in front of her bed was a huge window with millions of panes and framed by gauzy blue-and-cream curtains. It had a view of the tennis courts and the swimming pool. There was also a small frozen pond and what looked like a formal garden, covered with snow. It was absolutely beautiful.

"Why don't you sit down," Laurel suggested. "I'll be right out." She opened a gold-handled door in the corner of her room. Laurel even had her own bathroom. She had no idea

how lucky she was not to have to share a bathroom with her sister. But the more I thought
about it, the more I realized how lucky I was to
have Emily as my sister and not someone
stuck-up like Lana.

I sat down on the window seat beneath the
large window. There were a couple of old dolls
and stuffed animals also sitting on the blue
upholstered seat. Somehow, it was hard to picture Laurel Spencer playing with dolls or
stuffed animals.

"Okay," she said, coming back into the
room and shutting the bathroom door behind
her. "Let's get started. I thought that maybe we
could try something a little jazzy instead of
classical music or pop. What do you think?"
Laurel sat down cross-legged on the carpet in
front of the stereo.

"Well, what do you have in mind?" I asked.
I usually listen to the Top Forty stuff and I've
always loved classical music, but I know absolutely nothing about jazz.

Laurel leafed through her albums and
pulled one out. "Listen to this," she said,
putting it on the turntable.

The music was interesting. It was soothing

and exciting at the same time. It made me feel like flying. "I really like it," I said enthusiastically.

"Yeah?" Laurel replied, obviously pleased. "It's called 'Breezes Blowing' and it's one of my favorites. Listen to this part coming up. The tempo changes a lot, and I think we could use that to do some really cool things in the routine."

I got off the window seat and sat down next to her on the carpet. I listened carefully. She was right. "Oh, Laurel, this is beautiful! I think we should definitely use this one," I told her.

"I think so, too, but I also think we should listen to a few more things, just to keep our options open," she continued.

Besides Winslow, the class genius, Laurel is the only seventh grader I knew who says stuff like, "just to keep our options open." It didn't bother me today, though. Before I knew it, she had pulled out another album. "This is the music Katarina Witt used when she won the 1988 Olympics," Laurel said with this intense look on her face.

"Oh, yeah," I replied. "I loved her routine. I'd die to be able to skate like her."

Laurel nodded and smiled. "I know what you mean."

She put on a few more songs, but I didn't like any of them as much as the first song she had played. It was definitely the most unusual and the most fun.

"You know," Laurel said, putting it back on so we could listen to it again, "Lana did a dance to this last year, her freshman year at college. You'd think I would hate it, but . . ." She just left the sentence hanging. She got this sort of faraway look in her eyes, and then she shrugged, looking embarrassed. "Anyway," Laurel continued, getting up off the floor and walking to her closet, "the coach didn't say anything about costumes, but I've got this skating outfit in here somewhere . . . ." Laurel's voice trailed off as she disappeared inside the closet.

Her closet was almost the size of my bedroom. My entire wardrobe, plus my mother's and even my sister's would fit in that one closet, which was filled only with Laurel's stuff. From where I was sitting I could see tons of clothes. Some even had the tags still hanging on them.

Finally, Laurel emerged, holding a little sequined one-piece skating outfit. It was electric-blue and really cute. "I thought we could get two of these," Laurel said. "This one is a bit small, but I'm sure we can find two more just like it."

"That's great," I said, swallowing hard. I didn't exactly have the money to buy an outfit like that, but maybe Bradley would supply us with costumes.

"My sister is a ballet dancer, as you could probably tell," Laurel said, her voice getting tight again all of a sudden. "My mother is always buying her new outfits. She could probably pick something up for us, too."

"Sure," I replied, but not too enthusiastically. I was sure that whatever Mrs. Spencer picked out would be way too expensive for me.

Laurel looked at her watch. "I'm hungry," she said suddenly. "Let's go downstairs and get something to eat, okay?"

"Okay," I answered quickly. Now, that was an idea I liked. I was starved.

Laurel hung the skating outfit up in her closet and I followed her down a back staircase that led to the kitchen.

The Spencers' kitchen was also huge and really beautiful. It looked as if it came straight out of one of my mother's decorating magazines. The entire back wall was glass, with sliding doors on one end that opened onto a beautiful stone terrace. It overlooked the backyard, tennis courts, and pool. I also noticed something that looked like a stable in the distance.

I sat down at the big table while Laurel went to the refrigerator to find something to eat. "Oh, look, Edna, our housekeeper, left an apple pie, and nobody's even touched it yet!" Laurel exclaimed.

She brought the pie, two plates, two forks, two glasses, and a container of milk over to the table. "It looks delicious," I said.

Laurel nodded. "Edna is an incredible cook," she said, serving me a huge slice. "She's been with us since I was born. It's hard not to get fat with her around."

I nodded, not knowing what to say. I couldn't even imagine what it would be like to have a housekeeper. It was even harder to imagine having a stranger living in my house.

We ate and talked about ice skating for a while. I was having a good time and I was pretty sure Laurel was, too. Then we heard footsteps coming toward us. Laurel tensed immediately. I looked up and saw Mrs. Spencer walk into the kitchen.

"Ah, there you are, Laurel," Mrs. Spencer said in her chilly voice.

"Yes, Mother," Laurel replied, her voice as cool as her mother's. "We were having some pie and discussing our skating routine."

"Yes, of course," Mrs. Spencer said. "I'm going out with Lana now to look at a new dance costume for her audition next week."

"Katie and I were just talking about picking out costumes, too," Laurel said. "Maybe if you see something . . ."

Mrs. Spencer wasn't really listening. Even I could see that and I hardly knew her. She was busy pouring coffee into a beautiful china coffee cup, and staring out the window.

"What?" she finally said, turning away from the window to look at Laurel. "How nice." She took a few sips of coffee, put the cup in the sink, and smoothed down her sweater. "I'll see you later. It was very nice to meet you,

Katie."

I smiled my polite "for adults only" smile again. "It was nice to meet you, too, Mrs. Spencer," I replied in my most proper voice.

Laurel wasn't smiling at all. She actually looked a little upset. I kind of understood why. I mean, the whole thing with Laurel's mother and her sister sort of reminded me of my sister and my mother. I know how hard it is to have a perfect older sister. What was hard for me to imagine, though, was that someone as smart and beautiful as Laurel could have the same problem that I do.

I didn't say anything to Laurel, of course. Especially since Laurel became even quieter and more reserved after her mother left. I just finished my pie and my milk. I told her it was getting late, and I called my mom to come pick me up.

Chapter Six

"So, what was it like? Tell me everything. Does she really have two tennis courts and a huge pool?" Sabs was full of questions on Monday afternoon at lunch. I could tell that Randy and Allison were pretty curious, too.

I shrugged. "Well, she does have two tennis courts and a pool, but of course, we couldn't go swimming or anything. It was covered with snow. Her house is huge, and totally gorgeous. It's like something out of a magazine. She has her own bathroom and a huge bedroom with a CD player and a canopy bed, and I've never seen so many clothes in my life," I told them, pausing to take a breath. "Plus, I think they've even got a stable."

"Well, was there a chauffeur and a butler and a cook and everything?" Sabs prodded, stealing a potato chip off my tray.

"Sabs," Randy said, laughing. "Laurel isn't

the daughter of a billionaire or anything."

Sabs looked a little hurt. "Well, her father is the president of the bank, and they are almost the richest family in Acorn Falls."

"Well, they do have a housekeeper," I continued, "but I don't know about the rest. I met Laurel's mother and her older sister, Lana. She's in college." I paused and took a bite of my grilled cheese sandwich.

"And?" Sabs prompted, looking eager.

"She's a ballet dancer, right?" Allison said, surprising me. "I saw her dance last year when I went to the ballet with my parents."

"Yep, and she's really pretty," I added. I didn't think it would be fair to Laurel to tell anyone about how Mrs. Spencer was totally into Lana and didn't really pay attention to Laurel at all. "So," I began, in order to change the subject, "how was your band rehearsal on Sunday afternoon?"

Sabs looked at Randy and they both cracked up. "Well, I think we need about six thousand more rehearsals before we sound anything like a band," Sabs moaned.

"Totally," Randy agreed, shaking her head.

"That bad, huh?" Allison asked.

"Wait a second, Al," Sabs said teasingly. "You're not gonna quote me on that or anything, are you? I mean, you're not going to print what I just said in the newspaper?"

We all looked at Allison. "Of course not," Al replied quickly. "I'm going to listen to a practice this week sometime, and I'll write about it then. Okay?"

"Suit yourself," Randy said with a shrug. "They're your ears."

Allison, Sabrina, and I laughed.

"So, who wants to go over to Fitzie's after school?" Sabs asked. Fitzie's is the Bradley Junior High School hangout. We all go there to eat ice cream and french fries and talk.

"I can't," Allison told her. "I have some interviews to do today."

"I can't, either," I said. "I've got practice right after school every day this week." I made a face. "If you guys thought the band was bad, you should have seen our synchronized skating rehearsal on Saturday!"

"You're kidding," Allison said, surprised. "You're an amazing skater, and Laurel's supposed to be pretty good, too."

"Yeah." Randy turned to me. "What went

wrong?"

I shrugged, and picked up my apple. "I'm not really sure," I explained slowly. "I think it's because Laurel and I don't exactly trust each other, yet." I sighed just thinking about it. "That can make synchronized skating pretty tough."

Randy shook her head. "I still think it would be better if they made Laurel and Stacy one team. You and Kim Kushner would be great together."

"Maybe," I said. "But I guess Coach O'Neal doesn't agree. So, I'm stuck with Laurel, and she's stuck with me." I didn't feel like talking about it anymore for some reason. I looked over at the clock. I noticed that the bell was about to ring any second. "She's not so bad, anyway," I added softly, standing up to get rid of my tray.

Randy looked at me and raised her eyebrows in surprise. "Not so bad? What are you talking about?!" she exclaimed. Of the four of us, Randy dislikes Stacy and her friends the most.

The bell rang just then, saving me from having to explain anything. I know that Randy would never understand what I meant about Laurel. Having a perfect older sister is hard enough, but having a perfect sister like Lana and a mother like Mrs. Spencer must be next to impossible.

"Well, we'd better get going," Allison said, standing up, "or we'll be late for class."

"Katie," Randy said, suddenly serious, "remember when Allison and Stacy had that modeling job together? Remember how nice Stacy was to Al at first?"

I remembered. Allison had been the only other girl from Acorn Falls chosen to be a model, and Stacy had started treating her as if they had always been best friends. Then Stacy found out that one of the boys at the photo session liked Allison — and Stacy decided to steal him for herself. But I knew that Laurel would never do anything like that. Laurel was different.

"Randy, I really don't think that Laurel would do something like that," I told her.

"Just be careful, okay?" With that, Randy picked up her books and walked out of the cafeteria.

After school I walked over to the arena for

practice. I was the first one there, so I put my skates on and started warming up.

Laurel and Kim walked into the rink a few minutes later and we started working on the drills again. It went much easier this time, since Laurel was working with me. Coach O'Neal had a big smile on his face when he called us over to ask if we'd chosen our music. He told us to start working out some ideas for our routines on the ice while he listened to the tapes on his Walkman.

"I am absolutely exhausted," Laurel said after we had been skating for about an hour. I had to admit that I was pretty tired, too. "Let's sit down for a while," she suggested.

The two of us walked over to the bleachers and sat down.

I looked over at Stacy and Kim. Kim is an awesome figure skater. She's obviously experienced and she has a lot of good moves. Stacy was being her usual showy self, and it sort of worried me. Underneath all of the flashy moves she was making, Stacy's skating technique wasn't very good. I wondered if judges notice stuff like that.

"Come on," I said, turning to Laurel, who

was also watching them. "Let's go back. We've got a lot of work to do."

Laurel nodded. We skated to the corner of the rink. Soon Coach O'Neal came over with our tape.

"Laurel, Katie, I think you made a really good choice with this music," he said. "It's unusual and exciting, just the kind of thing I was hoping for. And you've improved a lot since Saturday. Good work." He gave us the tape and a little battery-operated radio, telling us to play the tape quietly while we worked out our routine.

We were concentrating so hard on choosing movements to match the music — with Coach O'Neal's help — that I lost track of everything that was going on around us. I could tell that Laurel had, too. She rewound the tape to the section with the abrupt transition from slow to fast. We started off skating side by side, each with one leg stretched out behind us, our arms extended wide. Then we started drifting apart and skating faster. We both did a quick turn and started back toward each other, crossing paths just as we were about to collide.

We kept drifting in and out like that, each

of us doing half of a figure eight, until both of us had built up enough speed to do a simultaneous single axel. Right after we landed, we each leapt into the air again, then crisscrossed back to the center of the ice and did a sit spin, stopping with our hands barely touching.

Suddenly, Laurel and I heard the sounds of whistling and clapping. We stopped dead in our tracks, and turned around. It was the high school boys' hockey team, cheering us on from the bleachers. I must have been beet red, but I had to admit that I felt really good. I glanced over at Laurel, and I could tell that she was happy, too.

Then I looked over at Stacy. She was furious! The perfect smile she usually wore while she was skating had turned into an angry scowl. She took off in a really complicated part of their routine, and Kim followed behind. It was obvious that Stacy was trying to show off. Suddenly, Kim lost her balance and stumbled. She knocked into Stacy and the two of them landed in a heap on the ice. Laurel and I looked at each other and closed our lips tightly to keep from giggling.

Finally, the coach blew his whistle. We all

got off the ice, followed him into the bleachers, and sat down around him.

"Well, girls," the coach began, "you've all improved two hundred percent from last week. You just have to try to work together a little more. That's the key to this kind of skating." He looked down at his clipboard. "That's it for today. Katie and Laurel, you're all set with music for your routine. Kim and Stacy, as I mentioned, you'll have to choose between the two tapes you brought in or decide on a third piece. Unfortunately, Bradley can't afford to give you costumes this time around — maybe next year. So you'll have to make or purchase your own costumes. Please start thinking about what you plan to do and let me know by next Saturday."

Laurel and I looked at each other. Then she whispered, "Don't worry, we'll figure out something." I nodded okay to her, then turned back to the coach.

"Does anybody have any questions?" He paused and waited for us to say something, but nobody did.

"Okay, then, I'll see you all on Wednesday. Tomorrow's rehearsal is canceled because I have to go out of town. That's it."

"Katie!" someone suddenly called from behind me. I turned to see Allison, Sabs, and Randy walking toward me.

"Hi, guys! What are you doing here?" I asked.

"I'm here to do a story on the skating teams," Allison explained. "We thought we'd all come over early so we could see you practice."

"That jump was awesome," Randy added. "You make skating look almost as easy as skateboarding." Skateboarding happens to be Randy's favorite hobby — next to playing the drums.

"Thanks," I said, smiling. "Laurel and I are really starting to work well together." I looked over at Laurel, who was sitting next to me. Just then Stacy walked up with Eva and B.Z. following right behind her.

"So, how's it going?" Stacy asked, turning to Laurel. "I guess it's obvious how well Kim and I are doing."

"It sure is!" I laughed, looking at Kim, who was glaring at Stacy. Maybe Stacy thought they were working well together, but it sure didn't seem like Kim thought so.

I saw Randy start to say something, but I put my hand on her sleeve to stop her. I wanted to deal with Stacy myself this time.

"I guess it's hard for the two of you, since your styles are so different," Stacy went on, ignoring my comment. "I mean, hockey players are so much . . . rougher and less polished than figure skaters. It's just too bad, Laurel. You might have had a chance at winning if you had been my partner."

"Cut it out, Stacy," Laurel retorted, standing up and looking at Stacy angrily. "Katie is an awesome figure skater, and you know it! You're just jealous, that's all!"

My mouth dropped open in surprise and I heard Sabrina gasp. I could not believe that Laurel "Ice Queen" Spencer was actually angry! I also couldn't believe that she had stood up for me in front of Stacy and her group! I mean, Laurel usually agrees with whatever Stacy says. Stacy looked pretty shocked, too. She turned on her heel and stomped off, Eva and B.Z. right behind her.

I didn't know what to say to Laurel. She was staring after Stacy with a shocked expression on her face, as if she couldn't believe what she had just done.

"Um . . . Katie," Sabrina said hesitantly, "Randy and I have to go back to school for our rehearsal now. We'll see you tomorrow."

"Yeah," Randy said, her expression puzzled as she looked at Laurel.

"And I have to go talk to the hockey coach," Allison added. "We'll see you later."

"Bye, guys. Thanks for coming to watch," I said. The three of them walked away, leaving Laurel and me standing there all by ourselves.

"Laurel," I began quietly, "thanks for doing that."

Laurel looked up from unlacing her skates, gave me a sort of half smile, and then looked down again.

I finished changing into my boots, put on my jacket, and headed outside. It was getting really dark. I knew that my mother was at a meeting and Emily was at the library with some friends, so I couldn't call home for a ride. I hate walking in the dark. It always gives me the creeps, even though I know that Acorn Falls is probably the safest place in the world.

Just as I was about to cross the parking lot,

a little red sports car pulled up. I heard the rink door slam shut behind me. I turned around and saw Laurel coming out. She walked across the parking lot to where I was standing.

She looked at me standing alone in the dark. "Umm . . . would you like to come back to my house to talk about the routine some more? My sister's here to pick me up," she said, looking over at the sports car.

"Sure," I replied. Now I wouldn't have to walk home alone in the dark. Anyway, after what had happened at the rink, I was starting to like Laurel more and more. No matter what Randy said, I knew that Laurel was different from Stacy.

"Okay," she said. Then Laurel smiled at me. She actually looked glad that I had said yes! We ran over to the little red car and I squeezed into this area behind the front seat that felt more like the trunk than any sort of backseat.

"Katie's coming over to work on our routine," Laurel told Lana.

Lana looked in the rearview mirror and smiled at me. I can't explain it, but her smile was really weird. Her mouth moved, but her eyes didn't light up at all. It was as if she was looking through me instead of at me.

Lana and Laurel did not say one word to each other — or me — during the whole ride home. Lana didn't even ask how practice had gone or anything. Even "Princess Emily" would have asked me about the routines and stuff. I guess Lana is so into herself that she doesn't care about anything or anyone else, not even her own sister.

When we finally got to the Spencers', Mrs. Spencer was in the study, sitting behind a huge mahogany desk with a pair of gold reading glasses on her nose. As soon as she heard us, she closed the book she was writing in and took off her glasses.

"Hello, girls," she said stiffly.

"Hi, Mother," Laurel replied, just as stiffly.

"Hello, Mrs. Spencer," I put in politely.

Mrs. Spencer just nodded, the gold chains around her neck jingling together. "Lana!" Mrs. Spencer called, looking past us. I turned around. Lana was in the hallway, peering at herself in a huge gilt-framed mirror. She came sweeping in gracefully as soon as Mrs. Spencer called.

"Yes, Mother?" she answered in the same formal tone.

"Lana," Mrs. Spencer continued, getting up from the desk. "I've been thinking about who to invite to your recital on Friday."

"Come on, let's go up to my room," Laurel said, turning around abruptly. I followed her up the stairs to her room.

We dumped our backpacks on the floor and Laurel closed the door. Then I called my house to see if my mother was home yet. Emily answered and said that she'd tell Mom where I was and that I should call when I wanted to be picked up. After watching that chilly exchange between Lana and Mrs. Spencer and the way they totally ignored Laurel, I realized that Emily and Mom weren't so bad.

"So," Laurel began, trying to sound cheerful, "I think we did pretty well today. What do you think?"

"Yeah," I agreed, sitting down on the carpet by Laurel's stereo system. "I think we have a chance to do really well."

And then there was this long silence. I don't know exactly why, but I decided to take a chance and tell her about me and "Princess

Emily." I thought that maybe it would make her feel better somehow.

"You know," I ventured, pretending to leaf through her albums while I was talking, "my sister, Emily, reminds me a lot of Lana."

"What do you mean?" Laurel asked, staring at me.

I took a deep breath. "Well, like, they're both really pretty and really smart and good at just about everything they do."

"But does your mother love your sister more than she . . ." she began, and then stopped herself.

"My mother thinks Emily is terrific," I said and giggled. "And sometimes I think she wishes she had two Emilys."

At first, Laurel just looked at me. But then she giggled, too. "You know, it drives me crazy that Lana is so good at everything," she said, sitting up on her bed. "That's why I love ice skating. It's something that Lana doesn't care about."

I shook my head. "I know what you mean," I agreed. "My sister would never dream of trying out for the ice hockey team."

"It's hard to believe that someone else is

going through the same thing that I am," Laurel said with a smile.

I suddenly realized that maybe Laurel wasn't stuck-up at all — she just seemed that way. If my family was as stiff and formal as Laurel's, I probably wouldn't be too friendly, either.

Anyway, I had to admit that I was starting to like Laurel. It was especially great to be able to talk about Emily and my mother to somebody who could really understand. I mean, Sabs is a younger sister, too, but it's different because she only has brothers.

"You know, Katie," Laurel said. "I was thinking that maybe Saturday would be a good day to go to Widmere Mall and look for our skating outfits. Are you free?"

"Sure," I replied. Wow! I never thought I would be spending this much time with Laurel Spencer, the "Ice Queen!"

Chapter Seven

Sabrina calls Katie.

EMILY: Hello? Campbell residence.

SABRINA: Hi, Emily. This is Sabrina Wells.
           Is Katie there?

EMILY: Just a minute.

(Emily puts the phone down and calls Katie.)

KATIE: Hello?

SABRINA: Katie, hi! It's me, Sabrina.

KATIE: Hi, Sabs.

SABRINA: Listen! Today at band practice,
           Mr. Metcalf asked if anyone
           wanted to help work on the deco-
           rations for the Winter Carnival
           Dance. I figured that since we did
           such a good job with the dance at
           the beginning of the year, the
           four of us could do it again.
           So I —

KATIE: You volunteered us to be on the

	decorating committee?
SABRINA:	Yeah! Randy signed up with me. I have this really cool idea for —
KATIE:	Sabs, I hardly have enough time to do my homework now with rehearsals and stuff. I don't think I can be on the decorating committee, too.
SABRINA:	Oh, Katie, it won't take much time at all. We can work out the ideas during lunch period and then we can make everything on the weekends or after school.
KATIE:	I guess so . . .
SABRINA:	Great! It wouldn't be any fun without you. Hey, do you want to go to the mall with me on Saturday? I finally saved up enough to buy a pair of those cool faded jeans with the rolled-up cuffs at the bottom.
KATIE:	I . . . I'd love to go, Sabs, but I can't.
SABRINA:	Oh. Do you have practice?
KATIE:	No, it's just that I'm already going to the mall.

SABRINA: So, what's the problem? I'll just meet you there, then.

KATIE: Well, I'm kind of going with someone else.

SABRINA: You are? With who?

KATIE: With Laurel.

SABRINA: Laurel?

KATIE: Yeah. We have to pick out our skating outfits for the carnival.

SABRINA: Oh.

KATIE: Maybe we can go some other day instead. How about tomorrow, after school? My skating practice got canceled.

SABRINA: I can't. I have band rehearsal. Don't worry about it, Katie. I'll ask Allison and Randy if they can come with me on Saturday. See you tomorrow.

KATIE: Bye.

Sabrina calls Randy.

RANDY: Hello, Randy Zak speaking.

SABRINA: Hi, Randy. It's me, Sabrina.

RANDY: Hey, Sabs! What's up?

SABRINA: I'm worried about Katie.

RANDY: Worried? What do you mean?

SABRINA: Well, I just called to tell her about the decorating committee and everything and I practically had to force her to say she'd do it!

RANDY: (*Laughing.*) Well, Sabs, you didn't exactly ask her if she wanted to be on the decorating committee. And she is pretty busy with her rehearsals.

SABRINA: I know. But then I asked her if she wanted to go to the mall with me on Saturday and she said she couldn't. She's already going with somebody else — Laurel Spencer!

RANDY: Laurel! Why is she going shopping with her?

SABRINA: She said they were picking out costumes for the carnival. Oh, Randy, what if she's going back into Stacy's group? What if she doesn't want to be friends with us anymore?

RANDY: Katie wouldn't do something like that. Calm down, Sabs. I'm going

to call Al and ask her what she
thinks. Now stop worrying! *Ciao!*

SABRINA: Bye, Ran.

Randy calls Allison.

CHARLIE: Hey, dude!

RANDY: Hi there, Charlie! Is Allison
home?

CHARLIE: Kowabunga, dude!

ALLISON: *(In the background, "Charlie! Give
me the phone!")* Hello?

RANDY: Hey, Al. It's Randy.

ALLISON: You sound really serious.

RANDY: I just talked to Sabs and she's
worried about Katie.

ALLISON: What's wrong with Katie?

RANDY: Well, Sabs said she didn't sound
all that happy to be on the decorating committee with us and
then she told Sabs that she
couldn't go to the mall with her
on Saturday because she's going
shopping with Laurel Spencer to
pick out their costumes instead.

ALLISON: Well, Katie is really busy right
now, and she and Laurel do have

	to pick out their costumes.
RANDY:	I know all that, but Sabs is worried that Katie might want to spend more time with Laurel than she does with us.
ALLISON:	You know, I did hear the coach telling them how important it is for them to get to know each other so that they can work well together. Maybe they're just spending a lot of time together so they have a better chance of winning the competition.
RANDY:	Maybe.
ALLISON:	Well, why don't we just ask Katie about it tomorrow at school.
RANDY:	I guess so, Al. Hey, you're right. Let's just ask her. Thanks, Al, I'm going to call Sabrina back right now and tell her what you said. *Ciao*, Al.
ALLISON:	Bye, Randy.

Chapter Eight

When I woke up the following morning, I remembered that I had a grammar quiz in English. I hadn't even started studying for it! Luckily, I'm pretty good at English, especially grammar, but I really didn't want to take a chance at ruining my A average in English. I ran to school to get a head start on studying. As the morning flew by, I looked at my English book whenever I could. Before I knew it, it was third-period English, which is also my home-room, and Ms. Staats was handing out the quiz. I put my book under my chair, took a deep breath, and started answering the questions.

After what seemed like forever, the bell rang and it was time for lunch.

"Whew," I said, sitting down in the cafeteria with Randy, Allison, and Sabs "I hope I did okay on that quiz."

77

Randy looked up at me, a puzzled expression on her face. "What do you mean? You always get A's in English."

"I know," I told her, "but I completely forgot about the quiz until this morning."

Sabs, Al, and Randy exchanged glances.

"Is something wrong?" I asked my best friends. "You guys don't look very happy."

"It's nothing, really," Sabs said quickly. Then her face turned pink. Her face always turns pink when she's not telling the whole truth about something.

"Sabs?" I asked, looking directly at her .

"Well, actually, we're kind of worried about you," Sabs blurted out.

"We haven't seen that much of you," Allison put in.

"And you've been spending a lot of time with Laurel Spencer," Randy scowled.

"You didn't want to be on the decorating committee with us," Sabs continued, "and now you're going shopping with Laurel instead of with us this Saturday and, well, we sort of . . ."

They thought I was starting to like Laurel more than I liked them! I couldn't believe it! Then I realized what I must have sounded like when I said I wasn't sure about being on the decorating committee with them and then told Sabs that I was going shopping with Laurel.

"Hey, guys," I said quietly. "We've all been really busy and it's been really hard to spend time together. But that doesn't mean we're not friends anymore." I sighed. "Yeah, I know I've been spending a lot of time with Laurel lately, but she's my partner. Luckily, we've started to get along, so our routine is working out, too. But you guys are my best friends." I looked seriously at each of them.

"She did stand up for you in front of Stacy," Randy admitted.

"That was really nice of her," Sabs added.

"Maybe we should get to know her, too," Allison suggested.

"That's a great idea!" I exclaimed. "Why don't all of us meet at my house on Saturday after we get back from our shopping trips to work on the decorations for the dance? I'll ask Laurel to come over and help."

Randy looked doubtful. "I don't know," she said slowly.

"It'll be fine, Randy," I assured her, keeping my fingers crossed under the table. "No problem at all."

On Saturday morning about ten-thirty the phone rang as I was getting out of the shower. "Hello?" I answered on the fifth ring.

"Hi, Katie? It's Laurel."

"Hi, Laurel," I said while towel-drying my hair.

"I just wanted to make sure we were still going to the mall today," she said.

"Sure! My mom even said she'd give us a ride over to Widmere, since she's going shopping with my sister, Emily."

"Great, what time should I be ready?"

I thought for a minute. I had to do my hair and get dressed, and I wasn't sure if Emily and my mother were ready yet. "How about in an hour?" I figured that would give everybody enough time.

"Okay," Laurel said.

"I thought maybe you could come by my house after we finish shopping," I suggested quickly. "Some friends of mine are coming over to work on decorations for the Winter Carnival Dance and I thought maybe you'd like to help." I waited for a second.

"That sounds like fun," Laurel answered at last. I let out the breath I hadn't even known I was holding.

"Great!" I exclaimed. "See you later." I hung up, went into my room, and closed the door behind me. I sat down on the end of my bed and combed out my hair, and then I went over to my closet. I picked out a pair of navy-blue pleated corduroy pants, a blue-striped button-down shirt, and a white sweater. I put my hair in a ponytail with a blue-and-white bow, pulled on my sneakers, and I was ready to go.

"Katie! Let's get going!" "Princess Emily" yelled.

I ran downstairs, hoping that my mother hadn't looked in my room on her way down — I hadn't even made my bed yet.

We got into the car, Mom and Emily in the front and me in the back. "Don't forget, we've got to pick up Laurel," I said.

"I remember," Mom replied, pulling out of the driveway. She smiled at me in the rearview mirror and then turned to Emily. "So, where do you think we should start?"

"Well," Emily answered, "I thought we

could go to Karo's craft shop first and see what they have there. Maybe they have some rhinestones and sequins. If they don't, we can go over to The Sew What Shop."

Mom nodded. "That's a good idea. Between the two, we should be able to find what we need."

I sat in the backseat, thinking about my own costume. Maybe Laurel and I could make our own costumes, too. It sounded like it would be fun. Since I knew I couldn't exactly afford to buy anything fancy, it also made sense. We pulled up to Laurel's house and Mom honked the horn. Laurel came running down the front steps. She got into the backseat next to me.

I introduced her to my mother and sister. Mom and Emily said hello and then went back to talking about Emily's dress. Laurel and I sat and listened, not saying a word.

"Okay, girls, here we are," my mom exclaimed finally, stopping in front of Jones's department store. "I'll drop you two here, okay?"

"Great," I said, opening the door. "What time should we meet you?"

"Two o'clock," my mother said. "We'll be right here."

"Thank you for the ride, Mrs. Campbell," Laurel said as she got out of the car.

Mom turned and waved. "You're very welcome, Laurel."

Then Emily waved, and the two of them drove away. Laurel and I ran to get into the store and out of the cold.

"So," I said, unzipping my jacket, "where do you want to go first?"

"Well," Laurel said, "I thought maybe we could go over to Elena Roberts to see what kinds of outfits they have in there."

Elena Roberts is one of the more expensive stores in Widmere Mall. I already knew there was no way that I'd be able to afford anything in there. I didn't know how to tell Laurel that, though. "Okay, let's go," I said, trying to sound enthusiastic.

"Hi, Laurel," a pretty blond salesperson greeted her as soon as we walked into the store. The salesperson looked as if she was in college, and she had a great figure. She was wearing this beige unconstructed jacket, a cream silk blouse, and black pants. She looked really chic and sophisticated.

"Hi," Laurel said calmly. "We're looking for skating outfits for the Winter Carnival. Any suggestions?"

"Well," the girl said, floating over to a section of the store filled with exercise clothes and leotards. "We have all of these things. This," she said, pulling out a bright red outfit with ruffles and feathers, "just came in. It's from France," she added with a smile.

I thought it looked a little too flashy. Then I took a peek at the price tag. I gulped. Seventy-five dollars! Even if I had that much money, I wouldn't spend it on a skating outfit for one competition.

Laurel looked at the price tag, too. "No, actually, I don't really see anything here that I like," she surprised me by saying. "How about you, Katie?"

"Not really," I said, shaking my head, totally relieved.

"Thanks, Nancy. We're going to keep looking. Say hi to your parents for me," Laurel concluded, and we left the store.

"Can you believe those prices?" she said when we'd gotten outside. "I don't think we should have to pay that much for something we're only wearing once, do you? Lana loves to shop there. That's how I know Nancy. Let's go over to Jump and Stretch. I think they're having a sale." I smiled at her, and she smiled back. It was weird — and nice — how well we were getting along.

"You know," Laurel said as we walked over to the other end of the mall, "it's funny how things worked out, isn't it?"

"What do you mean?" I asked her, even though I sort of had an idea of what she meant.

"Well, at first I wasn't too psyched about being your partner, but, well, I think we're really doing okay now. How about you?"

I nodded. "Yeah, I think it's going to work out really well."

"And one more thing," she said, and then hesitated. She looked as if she was trying to find the right words. "About Stacy. I think she was just mad that we didn't get to be partners. That's why she was so obnoxious."

I knew that Stacy was also pretty jealous of how well Laurel and I skated together, but I didn't say anything. Laurel was trying to be nice and I did appreciate it.

"Anyway," she continued, "she's happy with Kim now. Yesterday she told me that she thinks she has a better chance of winning with Kim than she would have had with me."

I raised my eyebrows in surprise. "She said that to you?"

Laurel laughed at my shocked expression. "That's just how Stacy is."

I thought about that as we made our way to Jump and Stretch, an athletic clothing store. Randy, Allison, and Sabrina never would have said something like that to me. We support each other. I guess Laurel and Stacy have a different kind of friendship.

We went into Jump and Stretch and headed straight for the ice skating rack. It's a totally different kind of store from Elena Roberts. There are bright neon lights and loud rock music pumping from speakers on the walls. The salesgirls all dress in fluorescent leggings and big T-shirts.

"Hey, Katie," Laurel said, looking at a simple pink leotard. "Why don't we keep our outfits really simple. How about these pink leotards?" she asked. And before I had a chance to answer, she added quickly, "These matching pink-and-yellow skating skirts only cost ten dollars each on sale." She put the leotard and skirt together and held them up for me to see.

"I think they'll be awesome-looking. And we could make something special to wear on our hair — maybe rhinestone barrettes or something like that. Let's get these," I told her.

"Good. That's settled. Listen, I'm starving," Laurel said when we left the store with our bags. "Do you want to get something to eat?" She looked at her watch. "It's only a little after twelve."

"Sounds great," I said, always happy to eat something.

"Laurel!" somebody called, and we turned around. Walking up behind us, wearing a dark green shirt dress, was Stacy Hansen, closely followed by Eva Malone and B. Z. Latimer.

Chapter Nine

"Hi, Stacy," Laurel said. "What's up?"

"Not much," Stacy replied, looking at me and smiling. "Hi, Katie."

"Hi," I said quietly. I didn't know how to act toward a Stacy Hansen who wasn't being obnoxious.

"I was watching you two in practice the other day," Stacy began. Suddenly, I knew exactly what was coming. "You looked pretty good."

My jaw dropped open. I glanced over at Laurel. She looked almost as surprised as I did. Was Stacy really complimenting us?

"I think everything worked out well, with the partners and everything," Stacy went on. "I like working with someone older." The way she said it, you would have thought that Kim was twenty-five or something instead of thirteen. I just smiled.

"Well," Laurel said hesitantly, "we were just going to get something to eat. Do you want to come?"

"I'm starved," Eva said. "Let's go over to Hamburger Local."

As the five of us walked toward the food court, B.Z. told us a funny story about her brother and his new girlfriend and their first date. Before I knew it, I was walking through the mall with Stacy Hansen and her friends, laughing so hard that I was almost crying.

Hamburger Local was completely packed, but luckily we didn't have to wait too long for a booth. I squeezed in first, and Laurel sat next to me, with B.Z. on the other side of her. Stacy and Eva sat across from us.

We all pulled out menus. "I'm going to have a super-deluxe burger with the works, large fries, and a strawberry shake," Eva announced.

"Eva, you are such a little pig," Stacy said, laughing. Eva, also laughing, threw a packet of sugar at her.

I have to admit, it was incredibly weird sitting in the mall having lunch with Laurel, B.Z., Eva, and especially Stacy. They were all gossiping and making fun of the other people in the restaurant. Some of the things they said were pretty mean. I looked at Laurel, wondering how we could have so much in common — like skating and our families and stuff — and still be so totally different.

Sitting there, I began to wish I were with Sabs, Randy, and Al instead.

"So," Stacy said after we'd ordered, "your friend Allison Cloud interviewed us yesterday for the school paper. Although I wouldn't exactly call it an interview. I've never seen anyone so nervous. I can't wait to see the articles she writes."

"Allison is an incredible writer," I said, defensively. "She's just shy sometimes."

Right then, the waitress came with our food. I was really glad. I wanted to eat and leave before one of them tried to insult one of my friends again.

"Listen," I said to Laurel after I had eaten my burger and fries in record time. "I think we'd better get going."

"Yeah," Laurel said, wiping her mouth with a napkin. "We've still got to go over to that crafts store."

"A *crafts* store?" Stacy asked, a snotty smile on her face.

"When did you get into crafts?" Eva asked, and then the two of them started laughing.

Laurel just smiled and we got out of the booth. "I'll see you guys later," she said.

"Katie, I'm really sorry about what Stacy said," Laurel commented after we'd paid our bills and walked out into the mall. "I guess she's still a little mad."

I nodded. It wasn't Laurel's fault that Stacy had been so mean.

We had reached the crafts store and went inside. We walked around for a while and then stopped in front of a large display. "How about these?" I said, picking up a few packages of rhinestones. "I think they'll look great against the pink leotard."

Laurel nodded. "Definitely. Let's buy them."

We also bought a couple of packages of sequins. Then we realized that it was two o'clock and time to meet my mother.

When we got in the car, my mom asked us if we had any trouble finding costumes.

"No," I told my mother excitedly. "We

found pink-and-yellow skating outfits and then we bought rhinestones and sequins to make fancy hair barrettes. Mom, will you help us with them?" I knew I was talking a mile a minute, but I couldn't help myself.

"Of course, dear. I'd be happy to. Why don't you and Laurel think about the way you'd like the barrettes to look and then we'll see what the three of us can do."

For the rest of the way home Emily kept talking about how gorgeous her silver dress was going to be. Laurel and I just looked at each other and smiled. It was definitely neat to be hanging out with someone who understood the older sister situation.

. When we got back to my house, it was almost two-thirty. Randy, Allison, and Sabrina were all supposed to be coming over around three o'clock. Mom checked with Laurel and me to see if we needed help. After we told her we were okay, she and Emily went down to the workroom in our basement. Laurel and I sat at the kitchen table to design the pattern we wanted to put on the barrettes.

"I think we should keep it really simple," I said as we sorted through the packages.

"That's a good idea," Laurel replied. "What do you think would be best?"

I looked at the small piles of sequins and rhinestones in front of us. "Well, we could glue the ribbons to the barrettes . . ."

"Yes," said Laurel excitedly, "and then we could sew rhinestones and sequins on the ribbons, and braid the ribbons into our hair."

Already, I could picture the two of us, crisscrossing our way around the ice, with the ribbons glittering in our hair. "This is going to be awesome!" I exclaimed.

"Katie," Laurel said quietly. "I think we'll need a lot more sequins."

I looked at the rhinestones and sequins and started laughing. "And maybe just a little more help!" With that, Laurel laughed out loud. It was really nice to see her relaxed and having a good time.

All of a sudden, there was a knock on the door. I knew it must be Sabs, Randy, and Allison.

"Hi, guys!" I said, opening the door and ushering them into the kitchen. "How was your trip to the mall?"

"Hi, Katie," Sabs replied, pulling off her

hat. She smoothed her curly red hair. "The jeans I wanted were on sale, so I got this really cool shirt, too. It's bright blue with all these different-colored squiggles running through it. You'll absolutely die when you see it."

Allison adjusted her bright red sweater. "We picked up all of the stuff we need for the decorations, too," she told me as we walked into the kitchen.

"And my mom loaned us all the brushes and glue and stuff," Randy added, holding up a canvas bag.

"Great! Then let's get started," I said, sitting down next to Laurel at the table. Sabs, Randy, and Al looked at each other for a second.

"Hi," said Laurel quietly. She was putting the different piles of rhinestones and sequins into separate plastic bags. She wasn't really looking at my friends and it was easy to tell that she felt uncomfortable.

"Hello, Laurel," Allison answered, pulling out the other chair next to Laurel. "Thanks for coming over to help us."

"Yeah," Sabrina said, "we have a lot of work to do if we're going to be ready for the dance."

"Do you want to cut, glue, or paint?" Randy asked, offering scissors and a bottle of glue from her bag.

Laurel took a pair of scissors. "What's the theme?" she asked.

"Well, we're going to try to do a 'Winter Wonderland' sort of a thing," Sabrina explained, pulling out sheets of paper and oaktag. "But everybody always does that."

"Randy came up with a much better idea," I put in.

"We're doing the 'Winter Sky,' instead," Allison continued. "We're putting up the strings of white lights that the school uses every year at Christmas and we're making silver stars and white snowflakes to hang from the ceiling."

"One of the art classes is making a big papier-mâché moon," Randy told us as we started cutting out snowflakes and stars. "Then I'm going to rig one of the lights to shine from behind it, so it has that kind of glow the moon always does, you know."

"That sounds really cool!" Laurel exclaimed, obviously impressed.

We all started busily tracing and cutting.

95

No one said anything for a few minutes.

"Anybody hungry?" I asked after we had made a big pile of stars and snowflakes.

"Well," Allison said, "I'm kind of thirsty. Could I have a glass of milk?"

"Of course," I said, putting a huge plate of cookies on the table. I went over to the refrigerator, took out the milk, got some glasses from the cabinet, and started to pour. "Who else wants some?" I asked, looking at the group.

"I'll have some," Sabs said, getting up to help me.

"Laurel?" I asked.

She shook her head. "No, thank you." She continued to trace snowflakes.

I brought Allison her milk and sat back down.

"Oh, Katie! I almost forgot to tell you!" Sabrina called from in front of the refrigerator, where she was putting the milk away. "I was with Allison yesterday when she went to talk to the skating coaches at the rink. I was sitting on the bleachers while she talked to some of the speed skaters when I overheard Coach O'Neal talking to some woman about the synchronized skating team. Katie, you are absolutely going to die when you hear what he said!"

"The woman was probably Katherine Stuart," Allison told us. "You know, the woman who thought up synchronized skating."

"What did they say? Was it good?" I asked.

Sabs practically skipped across the kitchen. "It was better than good," she replied. "He said that you and Laurel have a really good chance of winning a medal at the Olympics! He said your routine is well thought out and that you work very well together. Isn't that awesome?"

I looked over at Laurel. The grin on her face was as wide as the one on my own. "Thanks, Sabs," I said. "That makes me feel a lot better."

"Yeah, but listen to what else he said," Sabrina rushed on. "The woman asked him about the other team, Stacy and Kim, and Coach O'Neal got all serious. He said sometimes it just takes longer for two people to start working well together. He said that one of the girls was trying to be an individual and that unless she started acting like part of a team, their chances weren't as good as yours."

"Yeah, well, we all know who that is, don't we?" Randy said, laughing. "It's too bad they couldn't have found somebody else for Kim to skate with."

I froze, suddenly realizing what we had just done. We had just been talking about "Stacy the Great" like we always do and we had all forgotten — just for a moment — that Laurel is one of Stacy's best friends.

I looked over at Laurel. She had stopped in the middle of cutting out a snowflake. Her face had gone kind of pale and she was staring straight ahead. The whole kitchen was completely silent while all of us tried to think of something to say. Laurel put the snowflake and the scissors down on the table.

"Laurel, I — " I began.

"Katie, I — " Laurel said at the same time. She cleared her throat and then continued. "I think I'd better get going. It's late and I have to be home in time for dinner," she said in that cold, formal voice that her mother and sister always use.

My heart sank. Maybe it had been a big mistake to invite Laurel over today. She obviously didn't feel any more comfortable with my friends than I did with hers. I just hoped I hadn't ruined our partnership.

I showed Laurel where the phone was so she could call for a ride home. I stood by the front door with her, trying to talk about our costumes, until her father drove up and she left.

Then I went back into the kitchen. Sabs looked at me, her face still a bright shade of red. "I'm really sorry," she said.

I smiled at her. "It's okay, Sabs. I know you didn't mean anything. So how many more of these do you think we need?" I asked, changing the subject and holding up a paper star.

Chapter Ten

I woke up around seven-thirty Sunday morning. I took a quick shower, then ran down both flights of stairs to the workroom in the basement. I had practice at eleven-thirty, and I wanted to work on the costumes for a while before I had to leave.

Halfway down the cellar steps, I heard the sounds of the sewing machine, whirring away.

"Emily? Is that you?" my mother called over the noise.

"No, Mom," I replied, reaching the bottom of the stairs and walking over to my mother's side. "It's me."

"Hi, honey. You're up early," Mom said, smiling at me. "Sit down and talk to me for a while."

I sat down on the big brown overstuffed couch that used to be up in the living room when Emily and I were little. My dad built the workroom for my mom when I got old enough to have my own room. Over the years, all of our old furniture has sort of moved down there until it looks more like a den than a workroom. It's a really cozy place.

"So, how are things going?" my mother asked.

"Okay," I answered.

"Just okay?" Mom persisted.

"Well, I . . ." I hesitated. I really wanted to tell my mother all about what had happened yesterday and how worried I was that my partnership with Laurel might be ruined. But it was hard to find the right words.

"You know," Mom said into the silence, "I was just thinking. It's not that I'm not interested in what you're doing, Katie. It's just that I don't know a lot about skating, so it's hard to ask you questions. I'm sorry about that."

"Don't be sorry!" I cried. "You're the best mom in the whole world!" I jumped up from the couch and gave my mother a hug. "So you don't mind that I play hockey and that I'm skating at the Winter Carnival Olympics?"

"Mind?" my mother asked, holding me at arm's length. "Katie, I'm so proud of you.

"So," Mom said with a laugh after I had given her another hug, "what's going on that's got you so worried?"

Sitting back down on the couch, I poured out the whole story of Laurel and Stacy and the partnership that I hadn't really wanted at first. I explained about gradually growing to understand Laurel and how well we had been working together. Then I told her all about what had happened the day before.

"So, I came down here to see if I could get something done on our barrettes," I finished. "I thought that it would help somehow."

"Maybe it will," my mother agreed. "Let's have a look at the designs. This is one area I understand!"

We both laughed and then settled down to work. Together, we spread the ribbons and barrettes out on the worktable and decided on the best way to arrange the rhinestones and sequins.

I told her all about our skating routine and everything. Emily came down about an hour later and kept "oohing" and "aahing" over the barrettes until Mom laughingly told her to go make us all some breakfast.

A few minutes after eleven, I walked into an empty, echoing skating rink. I was lacing up my second skate when I heard the rink door slam shut. Laurel walked in and saw me, hesitated for a moment, then came over and sat on the bleachers beside me.

"Hi," I said.

"Hi," she answered, not looking into my eyes.

"I'm glad you came early," I told her.

"My sister had a recital today, so she dropped me off before she left," Laurel explained, pulling off her boots.

"Well, I wanted to — "

"If it's about yesterday," Laurel interrupted, "I understand. I know your friends weren't trying to be mean, or anything. Stacy is just, well, different."

"No, they didn't mean anything by it — " I began again.

"It was just like what Stacy said about Allison yesterday at the mall. Stacy doesn't understand what it's like to be shy. She wasn't being mean, either," Laurel continued, pushing the end of her long ponytail over her shoulder.

"I know — " I tried once more.

"I just wanted you to know that I don't want it to change anything between us," Laurel cut in again. "I mean, I'm not upset with you or anything, and I hope you're not upset with me."

"Laurel, I'm not upset with you," I said, finally. "I've been worried ever since you left my house that you would be so angry that we wouldn't be able to skate together anymore."

"Phew," Laurel sighed in relief. "I'm so glad that's over!" She slipped off her jacket and threw it onto the bleacher seat behind us.

I laughed. "You were worried, too!"

"Of course I was!" she exclaimed, leaning over to start lacing up her skates. "You don't think I'm going to let anything stop us from winning that gold medal, do you?" She smiled up at me and we both started to laugh.

"Oh, yeah! I have something to show you," I said just as we were about to walk out to the ice. I picked up the plastic bag and handed it to her.

"What is it?" she asked, eyeing the bag curiously.

"Just open it," I told her.

Laurel sat back down on the bleacher and

opened up the bag. She looked inside, gasped, then pulled out a rhinestone-covered barrette with a pink sequined ribbon attached to it.

"Katie! It looks even better than I thought it would!" Laurel whispered.

"They're not finished yet," I said quickly. "Mom and I only did one ribbon. She thinks a couple of more ribbons on each barrette ought to do it. Maybe you can come over later in the week and we'll finish them together. "

"It really does sparkle," Laurel said wonderingly, holding the shimmering barrette up to the bright rink lights.

Suddenly, Coach O'Neal called from the center of the ice. "Laurel! Katie! As soon as you two have finished warming up, I want you to go all the way though your routine, nonstop. Kim and Stacy won't be coming in until one-thirty, so you'll have the whole rink to yourselves."

Laurel carefully put the ribbons and barrettes back into the bag and we walked out onto the ice together. I skated around, bending, stretching, changing speeds and directions, until I was warm and limber. I looked over at Laurel to see if she was ready. She nodded, and we skated toward the center of the ice to take our starting positions. Coach O'Neal pressed the "play" button on the rink music system and the first bars of "Breezes Blowing" filled the air.

For four minutes, I lost myself in the music and the flowing movements and sudden changes of our routine. I wasn't really paying attention to Laurel at all. I just knew she was there, where she was supposed to be, when she was supposed to be. When I reached out my hand to catch hers, it was there. Somehow, I felt as if we were even breathing in sync.

At the end, Laurel and I spun to a stop, hand in hand in the center of the ice.

"Girls," Coach O'Neal called from the sidelines, "you do that same thing next Saturday, and you'll win yourselves a medal!"

Chapter Eleven

The next five days positively flew by. Stacy and Kim, instead of getting better, seemed to get worse. Stacy had picked out these expensive black, red, and gold outfits for the carnival without asking Kim. Kim said that there was no way she was going to wear one. Coach O'Neal finally had to step in and threaten to pick out their outfits himself. Meanwhile, they could barely get through even ten seconds of their routine without making a mistake.

Laurel and I worked on our skating routine every spare minute we had. We spent two hours after school each day perfecting each step. A couple of times that week Laurel came over to my house after practice and we continued to work. Sometimes Laurel stayed over for dinner and afterwards Mom would coach us on our posture and timing. Somehow the three of us would always end up laughing, we'd have so much fun.

Laurel and I agreed to listen to the music every night before we went to sleep. That way we could go over the timing of every movement. We also promised each other to watch ourselves in a mirror to make sure we held our arms, legs, and neck at exactly the right angles.

One day Emily surprised me with two pair of pink tights for Laurel and me to wear with our costumes. I thanked her and told her how much better they would look instead of the flesh-colored stockings we had planned to wear. Then another day Mom and I surprised Emily with a silver-and-blue tiara and matching earrings to go with her dress.

Sabs, Randy, Allison, and I got together on Tuesday and Thursday to finish up the decorations. The dance was on Friday after the pep rally, and we had all gotten excused from class to decorate the gym during sixth, seventh, and eighth periods on Friday. The art class that had made the papier-mâché moon helped us set everything up. After they had put the finishing touches on the moon, they made hundreds of stars and snowflakes just like ours, so the whole ceiling was full of them.

The strings of Christmas lights really did look like stars when we turned out the rest of the lights. But the best part of all was the big silvery moon. The spotlight Randy had set up behind it made a kind of shining halo all the way around.

Coach O'Neal kept Friday's practice short, just telling us to focus on our trouble spots. Laurel and I practiced the flying camels and the axels from our routine. Stacy and Kim had a fight over which parts they should practice and they were still arguing when Coach O'Neal told Laurel and me that we could leave.

I ran all the way home to shower, change, and eat dinner. I put on a really soft green-and-white angora sweater that I loved (a hand-me-down from Emily), a white wool miniskirt, tights, and green flats. I had even braided a green ribbon into my hair. After dinner, Mom dropped me off at school, where I was supposed to meet Randy, Allison, and Sabs.

"Hi, guys!" I called as I ran up to my three best friends. They were all standing in the hallway outside the gym.

"Hi!" Allison exclaimed, grinning. "Have you seen the school paper yet? The special edition for the Winter Carnival came out today, you know." She handed me a copy from the stack.

"'*The Bradley Voice* Winter Carnival Olympics Edition,'" I read out loud. "Where's your part, Al?"

"It's the centerfold," said Randy. "She wrote the articles, and did the layout and everything. It's awesome!"

I opened the paper up to the center. A big headline across the top said: GOOD LUCK TO ALL THE MEMBERS OF BRADLEY JUNIOR HIGH'S WINTER CARNIVAL OLYMPICS TEAM! There were pictures of some of the team members at practice, with little articles about each of the events, interviews with the team members and the coaches, and good-luck messages from other students and teachers at Bradley. It looked totally fantastic!

"Wow! This is really cool, Allison," I told her.

Sabrina pulled the clarinet reed out of her mouth. "Did you see the picture in the bottom right corner?" she asked.

"No," I answered, looking down at the bottom of the page. I gasped. It was a picture of Laurel and me at rehearsal, hanging in the air over the ice, big smiles on our faces, ponytails flying out behind. "Allison! When did you take this?"

"I asked Coach O'Neal to let one of the *Voice*'s photographers in while you were rehearsing on Sunday," she explained with a grin. "I have the original if you want it."

"I do," I assured her. Just looking at the picture gave me the shivers. Laurel and I looked almost professional!

"Let's go in," Sabs said, her voice quavering a little bit.

"You're not nervous or anything, are you?" I teased. Sabs always seems to get nervous before she performs in front of an audience, which is kind of funny, since she says she wants to be an actress.

"Well, we are the first thing on the whole program for the carnival, you know," Sabs said.

"Come on, Sabs," Randy said, walking toward the gym door. "It's time to get started."

"Good luck!" Allison and I called as we

watched them walk away.

At seven o'clock, the band started playing the school song. After they finished, the crowd gave them a standing ovation. I could see Sabs turning red again, even from where Al and I were sitting at the other end of the gym.

The dance was a lot of fun. I danced with Sam, Sabs's twin brother, a lot. For a couple of hours, I almost forgot that Laurel and I had to skate in the competition the next morning. But when it got to be nine-thirty or so, I remembered that I really needed to get a good night's sleep. I said good-bye to Sam, Sabs, Allison, and Randy and called my mother for a ride home.

The next morning I woke up suddenly, just before my alarm went off. Today was the day! I threw back the covers, scaring poor Pepper my cat half to death, and grabbed my robe from the foot of the bed. I was just about to race out the door to the bathroom for my shower when someone knocked.

I opened the door. Emily, her hair all tousled, stood yawning in the doorway.

"Good morning," I sang.

"Morning," she yawned. "I just wanted to

make sure you didn't oversleep."

"Thanks," I said, smiling at my sister.

"Good luck, Katie," Emily added. "I'll be there to cheer you on."

"Great," I said, happy that my sister would be in the audience. I was starting to wonder how I had ever thought that Emily wasn't a great sister.

Emily smiled and started walking back toward her own room. "Go ahead and take your shower. I'll help you do your hair when you're ready."

"Thanks, Em," I called over my shoulder.

By seven-thirty, I was sitting at the breakfast table, dressed and ready to go. Mom put a plate of scrambled eggs and bacon in front of me and all I could do was stare at it.

"You have to eat *something*," my mother urged.

"I can't!" I moaned. To my surprise, my mother laughed and took the plate away.

Mom drove me over to the rink a few minutes later. The only people allowed in were skaters and their coaches. The doors would open to the crowd at nine, after all of us had warmed up. I was expecting to walk into a quiet rink, but there were coaches and skaters from fifteen other schools scattered around the ice and the bleachers. I saw Coach O'Neal waving to me from one side of the rink, and I walked over to him.

"This is it, Katie!" he greeted me. "How are you this morning?"

"Nervous," I told him, sitting down to pull off my boots. He just smiled.

Laurel came in a few minutes later, her face white and her eyes huge. She sat down beside me without saying a word.

"I'm really glad we're skating first," I said, trying to make her feel a little better. "Then we can just do our best and not worry about how tough the competition is."

Laurel just nodded.

"Don't worry," I said quietly. "I know we'll do fine."

Just then, Stacy and Kim came in, dressed in the flashy costumes that Stacy had picked. Stacy walked right past us and sat on the bench on the other side of the coach. Kim stopped in front of us.

"I just wanted to wish you both good luck," she said, smiling. "You've got a great routine and you skate really well together. I'll bet you win the gold."

"Thanks, Kim," I said for the two of us. "Good luck to you, too."

"We're going to need it," she sighed. She walked over to sit down next to her partner.

Laurel and I moved out onto the ice and went through our warm-ups, staying out of everyone else's way as best we could. I noticed that our costumes were the simplest, but also the most unusual. Most of the other dresses were multicolored with braids or ruffles or fringes. I was really proud of the way we looked.

Then it was time to get off the ice. The bleachers were overflowing with people. I saw Randy, Sabs, and Allison holding up a huge sign that said: GOOD LUCK, KATIE AND LAUREL! My mother and sister were waving from a few rows behind them.

I heard someone start making announcements, but my heart was beating so loudly that I couldn't understand what was being said. Laurel and I were sitting down next to the coach, holding tightly to each other's hands. Then they played the National Anthem and called our names. In a blur of white ice and brightly colored, cheering crowds of people, Laurel and I were taking our places in the center of the ice.

"Good luck!" I whispered into the sudden hush.

"Good luck," Laurel whispered back.

For a minute, as the music started, I seemed to forget everything that I was supposed to do. Then my arm moved automatically above my head, and out of the corner of my eye I saw Laurel's arm doing the same. I realized then that it was going to be all right.

Just the way it had the week before, the music started to take me over. I could almost feel the breezes that the composer had felt when he wrote it, gently pushing and pulling me over the ice and into the air. I think I flew higher and farther in every jump than I ever had before, and Laurel was right there with me every step of the way. We landed together after each leap and axel; we turned and bent at the same moment.

It seemed as if we had started only seconds before when I realized that the song was over and Laurel and I were standing still again in the center of the ice. The noise from the crowd, which I hadn't heard until now, was suddenly totally deafening. Laurel and I hugged each other tight, waved to the crowd, and then skated off to sit and wait for our scores.

"For technical ability," the announcer began, "five-point-five, five-point-four, five-point-six, five-point-four, five-point-five, five-point-five.

"For artistic merit, five-point-eight, five-point-eight, five-point-nine, five-point-eight, five-point-eight, five-point-eight."

Laurel and I hugged each other. Our scores were really great! I crossed my fingers that they would be good enough to beat the team from Fennimer Junior High School.

Afterward, the only couples I could remember seeing were Stacy and Kim and a pair of girls in bright blue and green — the girls from Fennimer.

Stacy and Kim started off fine. I could tell that Stacy was trying to do what Coach O'Neal had told her to do just before they went out onto the ice: "Be a team member!" Then she started showing off again, lifting her arms a little higher, taking turns a little faster, and completely throwing off the timing. Kim tried to balance Stacy, but it was obvious that the two of them were just not skating in sync.

"Technical ability, four-point-four, four-point-five, four-point-four, four-point-four, four-point-five, four-point-five.

"For artistic merit, four-point-three, four-point-three, four-point-three, four-point-two, four-point-three, four-point-two," the announcer said impassively. Stacy's face turned white and Kim just walked away.

The team from Fennimer, two blond girls named Tara and Mary, were amazing to watch. They had picked a really popular dance song for their routine and they moved over the ice like blue-green lightning. The crowd went wild over them and I was totally positive that they were going to win.

They were the last pair of girls to skate and the judges took a long time to make their decisions. The ice rink staff were setting up a simple three-tiered platform on the ice for the awards ceremony. Laurel and I stood together at the side of the rink, holding hands again, both of us too nervous to talk.

"Technical ability," the announcer finally

said, "five-point-four, five-point-five, five-point-six, five-point-four, five-point-five, five-point-four. "Artistic merit, five-point-seven, five-point-seven, five-point-eight, five-point-nine, five-point-seven, five-point-eight."

I tried to do calculations in my head, but I was so excited that I couldn't figure it out. I knew that it was going to be very close, but all I could do was wait.

"Ladies and gentlemen, before I announce the names of the winners, the judges have asked me to tell you that this was a very tough competition. All of the young women who competed today deserve congratulations for their hard work and talent.

"Now for the results. In third place . . . from Widmere Junior High School . . . Michelle Baird and Tina Scott!" Two dark-haired girls in bright yellow outfits squealed and skated out to the platform, where Mr. Hansen presented them with the bronze medals.

"In second place . . . from Fennimer Junior High School . . . Mary May and Tara Peacock!" I cheered for the two girls as they skated out and got their medals.

"And last but not least, the first-place winners in Acorn Falls Winter Carnival Olympics synchronized skating competition . . . Katherine Campbell and Laurel Spencer!"

Suddenly, Coach O'Neal was pushing Laurel and me out onto the ice-shouting, "You did it! You did it!" over and over again. Then we were stepping up onto the highest platform at the center of the ice, bending down to let Mr. Hansen put a pair of gold medals around our necks, and being blinded by camera flashes from all directions. A few minutes later, we were surrounded by people shouting congratulations. I was in a daze until my mother and sister grabbed me into a bear hug, closely followed by Sabs, Al, and Randy.

. "Laurel!" I gasped. "We won! We did it!"

"I know!" she said, smiling. "I can't believe it!"

"Let's go celebrate!" Sabs called.

"Let's go to Fitzie's now, before the other events start," Randy suggested.

"I'll drive," my mother said, laughing.

"Come on, Katie!" Allison called.

I turned back to Laurel. "Are you coming?" I asked.

She looked over her shoulder, where Eva,

B.Z., and a few other people were standing around a completely furious Stacy.

"I don't think so," she said, turning back to me. "I think I should be with Stacy and those guys right now."

I nodded. At that moment, I wanted more than anything to be with my friends and family, celebrating. I knew that Laurel wanted the same thing.

"You know, I really wish our friends got along better," Laurel whispered to me.

"Me too," I replied. "But that doesn't mean we can't be friends, right?"

"Right!" Laurel agreed. We hugged each other. No matter what else happened, Laurel and I would always be friends after this, and that made me feel almost as good as winning!

Titles in the GIRL TALK series

⭐1 **WELCOME TO JUNIOR HIGH!** Introducing the Girl Talk characters, Sabrina Wells, Katie Campbell, Randy Zak, and Allison Cloud. When our four heroines meet and have to plan the first junior high dance of the year, the results are hilarious.

⭐2 **FACE-OFF!** Katie Campbell is just plain fed up with being "perfect." But when she decides to join the boys' ice hockey team, she gets more than she bargained for.

⭐3 **THE NEW YOU** Allison Cloud is down in the dumps, and her friends decide she needs a makeover, just in time for a real live magazine shoot!

⭐4 **REBEL, REBEL** Randy Zak is acting even stranger than usual — could a visit from her cute friend from New York have something to do with it?

⭐5 **IT'S ALL IN THE STARS** Sabrina Wells's twin brother, Sam, enlists the aid of the class nerd, Winslow, to play a practical joke on her. The problem is, Winslow takes it seriously!

⭐6 **THE GHOST OF EAGLE MOUNTAIN** The girls go camping, only to discover that they're sleeping on the very spot where the Ghost of Eagle Mountain wanders!

ODD COUPLE

★ 7 When a school project pairs goody-two-shoes, Mark Wright, with super-hip Randy Zak as "parents" of an egg, Randy and Mark find out that they actually have something in common.

STEALING THE SHOW

★ 8 Sabrina sets out to prove that she's perfect for the lead role in the school production of *Grease*, only to land herself in one crazy mix-up after another.

PEER PRESSURE

★ 9 Katie Campbell doesn't know whether to laugh or cry when Stacy the Great's best friend Laurel Spencer is chosen as her skating partner for the Winter Carnival.

FALLING IN LIKE

★ 10 Allison's not happy about having to tutor seventh-grade troublemaker Billy Dixon. But when they discover a key to his problems, Allison finds out that you can't always judge a book by its cover.

MIXED FEELINGS

★ 11 A gorgeous Canadian boy moves to Acorn Falls and life turns pretty interesting for Katie Campbell — especially when Sabrina likes the new boy and he likes Katie!

DRUMMER GIRL

★ 12 It's time for the annual 'Battle of the Bands'. Randy decides to start her own all-girl band after she overhears the guys in Acorn Falls say that girls can't play rock 'n' roll!

LOOK FOR THE GIRL TALK SERIES!
COMING SOON TO A STORE NEAR YOU!

TALK BACK!

TELL US WHAT YOU THINK ABOUT GIRL TALK

Name _____

Address _____

City _____ State _____ Zip _____

Birthday: Day _____ Mo _____ Year _____

Telephone Number (___) _____

1) On a scale of 1 (The Pits) to 5 (The Max), how would you rate Girl Talk?   Circle One:

1   2   3   4   5

2) What do you like most about Girl Talk?

___Characters___Situations___Telephone Talk

Other _____

3) Who is your favorite character?   Circle One:

Sabrina   Katie   Randy
Allison   Stacy   Other

4) Who is your least favorite character?

_____

5) What do you want to read about in Girl Talk?

_____
_____

Send completed form to :
Western Publishing Company, Inc.
1220 Mound Avenue Mail Station #85
Racine, Wisconsin 53404